She was paralysed by the heat in his eyes, warming her through from head to toe, settling in the pit of her stomach, awakening a sweet, insistent ache she hadn't felt for so long.

The naked desire in his face provoked pride, need, want.

And she wanted him too.

She'd wanted him since the moment he had sauntered into her office, arrogant and demanding, making her think and making her do and making her feel. Not just because he looked so good, was so tall and so broad and so solid, and not just because he had eyes that caressed and a mouth that made her knees tremble, but because he was a man who cared, hide it as he might.

But he was a man who was leaving. A man with itchy feet, who lived his life on the edge of civilisation, risking his life every day.

Right now it was hard to remember why that was a problem.

Dear Reader

I love fairytales—and I especially love it when they are given a twist: when the characters choose their own way rather than following the path laid out for them by their fairy godmothers.

Clara might spend her whole life working, but that's absolutely fine by her. Balls? Dresses? Glass slippers? Not for this reluctant Cinderella! Give her a mop, a duster and a spreadsheet any day—because if she buries herself in work she won't have time to notice how lonely she is. Until Castor 'Raff' Rafferty comes through her door and shows her just what she's been missing.

Tall, handsome, heir to a fortune…Raff leads a life that seems charmed, but it's a gilded cage. His future is all planned out: settling down, heading up the family business, giving up the dangerous but meaningful work he loves so much. Clara could provide him with some much needed time to plan his escape—if he could just persuade her to put down her broom and let him whisk her away to the ball…

When I first started thinking about Raff and Clara's story I spent a lot of time on the Médecins Sans Frontières website, reading the blogs written by staff in the field. The charity Raff works for is imaginary, but it is inspired by the amazing doctors, nurses and project managers who volunteer their time to work in some of the most dangerous and deprived places on earth, providing much needed healthcare. You can check out their stories for yourself at www.msf.org.uk

Love

Jessica x

HIS RELUCTANT CINDERELLA

BY
JESSICA GILMORE

Published in Great Britain 2014
by Mills & Boon, an imprint of Harlequin (UK) Limited,
Eton House, 18-24 Paradise Road, Richmond, Surrey, TW9 1SR

© 2014 Jessica Gilmore

ISBN: 978-0-263-24319-2

Harlequin (UK) Limited's policy is to use papers that are natural,
renewable and recyclable products and made from wood grown in
sustainable forests. The logging and manufacturing processes conform
to the legal environmental regulations of the country of origin.

Printed and bound in Great Britain
by CPI Antony Rowe, Chippenham, Wiltshire

After learning to read aged just two, **Jessica Gilmore** spent every childhood party hiding in bedrooms in case the birthday girl had a book or two she hadn't read yet. Discovering Mills & Boon® on a family holiday, Jessica realised that romance-writing was her true vocation and proceeded to spend her maths lessons practising her art, creating *Dynasty*-inspired series starring herself and Morten Harket's cheekbones. Writing for Mills & Boon® really is a dream come true!

A former au pair, bookseller, marketing manager and Scarborough seafront trader—selling rock from under a sign that said 'Cheapest on the Front'—Jessica now works as a membership manager for a regional environmental charity. Sadly, she spends most of her time chained to her desk, wrestling with databases, but likes to sneak out to one of their beautiful reserves whenever she gets a chance. Married to an extremely patient man, Jessica lives in the beautiful and historic city of York, with one daughter, one very fluffy dog, two dog-loathing cats and a goldfish named Bob.

On the rare occasions when she is not writing, working, taking her daughter to activities or Tweeting, Jessica likes to plan holidays—and uses her favourite locations in her books. She writes deeply emotional romance with a hint of humour, a splash of sunshine and usually a great deal of delicious food—and equally delicious heroes.

Recent books by Jessica Gilmore:

SUMMER WITH THE MILLIONAIRE
THE RETURN OF MRS JONES

**This and other titles by Jessica Gilmore
are also available in eBook format
from www.millsandboon.co.uk**

DEDICATION

For my parents

To Mum, thank you for weekly trips to the library,
for never telling me to 'put that book down',
for the gift of words and stories and dreams.

And to Dad for proving that families
are more than genes, that blood isn't thicker than water,
that nurture totally trumps nature—
and for being the best grandpa in the world.

I love you both x

CHAPTER ONE

'IF YOU TELL ME where my sister is, I'll give you ten thousand pounds.'

The down-turned head in front of him lifted slowly and Raff found himself coolly assessed by a pair of the greenest eyes he had ever seen, their slight upward tilt irresistibly feline, the effect heightened by high, slanting cheekbones and a pointed chin.

If this lady had a tail, it would definitely be swishing slowly. A warning sign.

He'd never been that good at heeding warnings. He liked to see them more as a challenge.

'I beg your pardon?' Her voice was as cold as her stare. Maybe he should have tried charm before hard cash, but somehow Raff doubted that even his patented charm would work on this cool cat.

Her dismissal should have annoyed him, he was used to people snapping to attention when he needed them, but he had to admit he was intrigued. He smiled, slow and warm. 'Clara Castleton?'

There was no answering upturn of her full mouth as she nodded at the name tag, displayed neatly on the modern oak desk. 'As you can see. But I don't believe you introduced yourself?'

'I don't believe I did.' Raff hooked the wooden chair

out from opposite her desk and slid into it. He knew his six-foot-two frame could be intimidating, used it to his advantage sometimes, but for some reason, standing before her incredibly neat desk, he was irresistibly reminded of being summoned to the headmaster's office.

Although that was where any resemblance to his long-suffering former headmaster ended despite her severely cut suit—her strawberry-blonde hair might be ruthlessly scraped back but it looked as if it was all there and she lacked the terrifying bushy eyebrows. Hers were rather neat lines, adding a flourish to what really was a remarkably pretty face, although the hair, the discreet make-up and the suit were all designed to hide the fact. Interesting. Raff filed that fact away for future use. He sensed he was going to need all the weapons he could get.

He leant back in his chair, keeping his eyes fixed on her face. 'Castor Rafferty, but you can call me Raff. I believe you know my sister.'

'Oh.' Her eyes flickered away from his searching expression. 'I was expecting you a couple of days ago.'

'I've been busy dropping everything and rushing back to England. So, are you going to tell me where Polly is?'

Clara Castleton shook her head. 'I wouldn't tell you if I knew,' she said. 'But I don't.'

Raff narrowed his eyes. He didn't believe her, didn't want to believe her. Because if she was telling the truth he was at an utter dead end. 'Come now, Clara. I can call you Clara, can't I? This short and simple email...' he held up his phone with the email displayed. Not that he needed to be reminded what it said; he knew it off by heart '...tells me quite clearly that in an emergency my sister can be contacted via Clara of Castleton's Concierge Consultancy. Nice alliteration by the way.'

She took the phone and read the message, those intriguing eyebrows raised in surprise. 'Sorry, I have an email address, nothing more.'

'I've tried emailing a couple of times.' Try ten. Or twenty. 'Maybe she'll read it if it comes from you,' he suggested hopefully. 'My original offer still stands.'

'Keep your money, Mr Rafferty.' Her voice was positively icy now. Raff was already finding the anaemic English spring chilly; her tone brought the temperature down another few degrees. 'Your sister has taken care of my fees. She asked me to help settle you in, to continue to make sure the house is cared for. This I can do, it's *what* I do. But unless there is a real emergency I won't be sending any emails.'

It was a clear dismissal—and it rankled, far more than it should do. Time for a change of tactic; he needed to get this right so Polly would be back where she belonged, managing Rafferty's, the iconic department store founded by their great-grandfather.

And he would be back in the field where *he* belonged. He'd barely had a chance to unpack, to assess what was needed, how to play his own small yet vital part in stopping the humanitarian crisis unfolding before him from becoming a full-blown disaster, when he'd received Polly's email ordering him home.

Typical of his family, to think their petty affairs were worth more than thousands of lives. And yet here he was.

Raff looked around the neat, organised room for inspiration. Such a contrast from his last office: a tent on the outskirts of the camp. Even the office before that, situated in an actual building, had been a small room, almost a cupboard, piled high with crates, paperwork and supplies. He couldn't imagine having all this space to himself.

Occupying the corner at the end of the quaint high

street, Clara's office took up the entire ground floor of a former terraced shop, the original lead-paned bow windows now veiled with blinds, the iron sign holder above the front door empty, replaced by a neat plaque set in the wall.

Outside looked like a still from a film set in Ye Olde England but the inside was a sharp modern contrast. The large room was painted white with only bright-framed photographs to alleviate the starkness, although through the French doors at the back Raff could see a paved courtyard filled with flowering tubs and a small iron table and chairs, a lone hint of homeliness.

Clara's very large and very tidy desk was near the back by the far wall, facing out across the room. Two inviting sofas clustered by the front window surrounding a coffee table heaped with glossy lifestyle magazines. The whole room was discreet, tasteful and gave him no clue whatsoever to its owner's personality.

Maybe it was time to try the charm after all.

Raff leaned forward confidingly. 'I'm worried about Polly,' he said. 'It's so out of character for her to disappear like this. What if she's ill? I just want to know that she's all right.' He allowed a hint of a rueful smile to appear.

The look on Clara's face oozed disapproval. Yep, she was still giving out the whole 'disappointed headmaster' vibe. 'Mr Rafferty, you and I both know that your sister hasn't just disappeared. She's gone on holiday after making sure that both her job and home are taken care of. There really is no mystery.

'It may be a *little* out of character.' Was that doubt creeping into her voice? 'I haven't known her to take even a long weekend before—but that's probably exactly why she needs this break. Besides, isn't it your company too?'

Unfortunately. 'Just what has my sister said to you?'

A faint flush crept over the high cheekbones. 'I don't understand.'

Oh, she understood all right.

'She didn't use the words irresponsible or lazy?' Polly's email might have been short but it had been to the point. *Her* point of view. As always, they differed on that.

The flush deepened. Not so cool after all. The colour gave her warmth, emphasising the curve of her cheek, the lushly dark lashes veiling those incredible eyes. An unexpected jolt of pure attraction shot through him. Before she had been like a marble statue, nice to look at but offputtingly chilly. This hint of vulnerability gave her dimensions. Unwanted, unneeded dimensions. He wasn't here to flirt. With any luck he'd hardly be here at all.

'Our communication was purely business,' but she couldn't meet his eye. 'Now, I do happen to have a half-hour free right now. Is this a convenient time for me to show you the house?'

No, Raff wanted to snap. No, actually it wasn't convenient. None of this was. Not Polly's most uncharacteristic disappearance, nor her SOS ordering him home right now. She couldn't expect him to drop everything and step in so she could go on some extended holiday.

Even though he hadn't been home in over four years. He pushed the thought away. He wasn't needed here, not as he was out in the field. Besides, his absence had given Polly the opportunity she had wanted; the two circumstances were entirely different.

Which made this whole disappearing act even odder. If he allowed himself to stop feeling irritated he might start getting worried.

'Mr Rafferty?'

'Raff,' he corrected her. 'Mr Rafferty makes me think I'm back at school.'

Or even worse back in the boardroom, sitting round a ridiculously large table listening to never-ending presentations and impenetrable jargon, itching to get up, stop talking and *do*.

'Raff,' she said after a reluctant pause. He liked the sound of his name on her tongue. Crisp and cool like a smooth lager on a hot summer's day. '*Is* now a convenient time?'

Not really but Polly had backed him into a hole and until he had a chance to work out what had happened he didn't have much choice.

He *was* still joint Vice CEO of Rafferty's, after all. Someone had to take over the reins, stop Grandfather working himself into an early grave; in Polly's absence that person had to be him.

She had planned it well. The contrary streak in Raff wanted to ensure she didn't get her way. To walk away from her home, her company. Show her he couldn't be manipulated.

But of course he couldn't. Despite everything Polly was his twin—and pulling a stunt like this was completely out of character. Polly didn't just quit; she was the hardest worker he knew. The sooner he found out what had happened and fixed it, the sooner they could both return to their lives.

And he was sure that the woman in front of him could help him, if he could just find a way to make her crack, like a ripe and rather inviting nut.

'Okay, then, Clara Castleton,' he said. 'Lead the way.'

'Is there something wrong?'

Clara knew she sounded cold. Raff Rafferty might

have turned on the charm but she preferred to keep a professional distance, especially when her new client owned
an easy smile and a devilish glint in blue, blue eyes.

And a disconcerting way of looking at her as if he
could see straight through her barriers, as if the suit
didn't fool him at all. Her skin fizzed with awareness of
his intense gaze—or with irritation at his high-handed
ways.

Either way he was dangerous. The sooner she settled
him in and got out, the better.

The tall blond man wasn't actually her client but his
sister had made sure Clara was fully briefed. The Golden
Boy, apple of his grandfather's eye. Clara knew men like
Raff Rafferty all too well. It wasn't a type she admired
at all. Not any more.

Look at him now, leaning against her van, a smirk
playing on those finely sculpted lips.

'This yours?'

Clara held up the keys. 'Why?'

His eyes swept assessingly over the large, practical
van, her logo and contact details tastefully picked out
on the side. 'I imagined you driving something a little
more elegant.'

Clara took a breath, an unexpected flutter in her stomach at the idea of something elegant, that she was fea-
turing in his imagination at all. She pushed the thought
resolutely away.

'Save your imaginings,' she said. 'The van is practical.'

'It's practical all right.'

His lips were pressed together; Clara had the distinct
impression that he was laughing at her. 'I'm sure it's not
your usual style,' she said as evenly as she could. 'If you'd
rather walk I can meet you there.'

'Don't worry about me. I'm not fussy.'

'Great.' She was sure that her attempted smile looked more like a grimace. She should make him sit in the back amongst the cleaning supplies and tools. See how fussy he was then.

At least, Clara reflected as she pulled the van out into the narrow main road that ran through the town, he hadn't offered to drive. Some men found it hard to be driven by a woman, especially in a large van like this. Raff was the very definition of relaxed, leaning back in his seat, lean jean-clad legs outstretched.

Practical it might be, but the large van always felt out of place on Hopeford's narrow windy streets. It took all Clara's skills and concentration to negotiate the small roads. The overhanging houses and cobbled pavements might be picturesque enough to pull in tourists and Londoners looking for a lengthy if direct commute, but they were completely ill suited for work vans.

And it was easier to concentrate on the driving than it was trying to make conversation with someone who seemed to suck all the air out of the van. It had always felt so spacious before.

Unfortunately Raff didn't seem to feel the same way. 'How long has Polly lived here?'

Clara negotiated a particularly tight turn before answering as briefly as was polite. 'About three years, I believe.'

He looked about him. 'It seems quiet, not her kind of place at all.'

Clara glanced over at him. She knew that he and Polly were twins and the relationship was obvious. They both had straight, dark blond hair, although his was far more dishevelled than his sister's usual sleek chignon, straight, almost Roman noses and well-cut mouths. But the similarity seemed only skin deep. Polly Rafferty was quiet, always working, whether at home or on her long train journey into the capital. She was reserved and polite; Clara was the closest thing she had in Hopeford to a friend.

On balance she much preferred the sister's reservation to the brother's easy charm and devilish grin. They were dangerous attributes, especially if you had once been susceptible to a laid-back rich boy's style.

Clara knew all too well where that led. Nowhere she ever wanted to go again.

'The town is increasingly popular,' she said, carefully keeping her voice neutral. 'It's pretty, we have good schools and we're on a direct train line into London.'

'Ye—es…' He sounded doubtful. 'But Polly doesn't have kids and last I saw she wasn't that bothered about quiet either. If she wanted pretty there are plenty of places in London that fit the bill. It's not like she's short of money.'

His tone was disparaging and the look on his face as he stared out at the picturesque street no better. Clara gripped the steering wheel tightly. She might moan about incomers flooding the place, driving prices up and her friends out, but at least they appreciated the town.

'You don't have to stay here,' she said after a moment. 'There are plenty of hotels in London.'

His lips tightened. 'The key to Polly's whereabouts is here. I can feel it. Until I know where she is—and how I can get her to come home—I'm staying.'

Polly Rafferty's house was just a short drive away from Clara's office, a pretty cottage situated on a meandering lane leading out to the countryside. It was one of Clara's favourite houses; many of her clients had bought the huge new builds that had sprung up on gated estates around the town, large and luxurious certainly but lacking in Hopeford charm.

'Picturesque.' It wasn't a compliment, not with that twist of the mouth.

'Isn't it?' she said, deliberately taking his statement at face value. 'This is the most sought-after area in town, close to the countryside and the train station. There's a good pub within walking distance too.'

'All amenities,' Raff said, looking about him, his expression one step removed from disdainful.

The condescension prickled away at her. It was odd. She had so many clients who talked down to her and her staff and it never got to her; twenty minutes in this man's sardonic company and she was ready to scream.

Ignoring him, Clara unlocked the front door and stood back to let the tall man enter. He stood there for a second, clearly conflicted about preceding her into the house. She waited patiently, a thrill of satisfaction running through her when he finally gave in, ducking to fit his tall frame through the small door.

He was as out of place in the low-ceilinged, beamed cottage as a cat at Crufts. The house was sparingly and tastefully decorated but the designer had worked with the history rather than against it. Rich fabrics, colour and flowers predominated throughout, a sharp contrast with the casually dressed man in jeans and desert boots, an old kitbag hoisted over his shoulder.

He didn't look much like a playboy. He looked like a weary soldier who wanted nothing more than a hot shower and a bed.

'The bedrooms are upstairs,' Clara said, gesturing towards the small creaky staircase that wound up to the next floor. 'I had the main guest room made up for you.

It's the second door on the right. There's an en-suite shower room.'

She should offer to show him up there but every nerve was screeching at her to stay downstairs, to keep her distance. Noticing the weary slant to his shoulders led to seeing the lines around his eyes, the dark hollows under them emphasising the dark navy blue, leading in turn to a disturbing awareness of the lines of his body under the rumpled T-shirt, the way his battered jeans clung to lean, muscled legs.

She squeezed her eyes shut. What was she doing ogling clients? *Pull yourself together.*

Maybe her mother *was* right: it might be time to consider dating again. Her hormones were clearly so tired of being kept under rigid control they were running amok for the most unsuitable of men.

Clara took a deep breath, feeling her nails bite into her palms as she tried to summon her habitual poise. 'The kitchen's through here,' she said, marching back into the hallway and leading the way into the light spacious room that took up the entire back of the cottage. She had always envied Polly this room. It was made for a family, not for one lone workaholic who ate standing up at the counter. She didn't look back as she continued to briskly outline the preparations she had made.

'I stocked up with the usual order but if there is anything else you'd like write it here.' She gestured towards the memo pad on the front of the fridge.

She turned to check if he was following and skidded to a halt, backing up a few steps as she nearly collided with his broad chest. 'Erm, there's a lovely courgette and feta quiche in the freezer, which will make a nice, simple dinner tonight.' Clara could feel the telltale burn spreading across her cheeks and knew she was turning red. She backed away another step, turning her back on him once again, finding safety in the sleek chrome fridge door. 'If you want your dinner provided then Sue, the regular cleaner, will pop a stew or a curry into the slow cooker for you but you must leave a note on the morning you require it or email the office before ten a.m.'

She was babbling. She *never* babbled but everything felt out of kilter. Her whole body was prickled with awareness of his nearness. She turned, smiled brightly. 'Any questions?'

Raff's mouth quirked. 'Is there anything you don't do around here?'

'Your sister employs me to keep the house clean, the cupboards stocked, to take care of any problems. She's a busy woman,' she said, unnaturally defensive as she saw the disbelief in his face. 'I offer a full housekeeping service without the inconvenience of live-in staff.'

'She pays you to stock the fridge with quiche?' But the smirk was playing around his mouth again. Annoyingly.

'My father's quiche,' she corrected him. 'Don't knock it until you've tried it. There's also plenty of salad, fruit and hummus.'

'Beer, crisps, meat?'

'Put it on the list,' she said, wanting to remain professional, aloof, but she could feel her mouth responding to his smile, wanting to bend upwards.

She needed to get out. Get some air and give herself a stern talking-to. 'The pub does food if you want something different,' she said. 'Or there are some takeaway menus on the memo board. You'll be fine.'

'I usually am.'

'Okay, then.' She paused, made awkward by the intensity of his gaze. With an effort Clara pulled on her professional persona like a comfort blanket. 'If you have any problems at all just get in touch.' She held out her card.

He reached out slowly and plucked it out of her hand, his fingers slightly brushing against hers as he did so. She jerked her hand away as if burnt, the heat shocking her. She swallowed back a gasp with an effort, hoping she hadn't given away her discomfort.

'I'll do that.' He was looking right into her eyes as he said it.

'Good.' Damn, she sounded breathless. 'That's everything. Have a nice evening.'

Clara began to back out of the kitchen, not wanting to be the one to break the eye contact. It was as if he had a hypnotic effect on her, breaking through her usual calm, ruffling the feathers she kept so carefully smoothed down.

'Ouch.' Something underfoot tripped her up and she put a hand out to steady herself, her eyes wrenched from his.

'Are you all right?'

'Yes, thanks.' Steadier in more ways than one, relieved to be free of his gaze. She looked down at the trip hazard, confused by the large hessian mouse. 'Oh, how could I forget? Mr Simpkins' usual routine is biscuits first thing in the morning and more biscuits and some fish in the evening. He has his own cupboard under the sink.'

'Mr Simpkins?' He sounded apprehensive.

'The man of the house.' She smiled sweetly. 'I do hope you like cats.'

And surprisingly cheered up by the horrified look on his face, Clara swivelled and walked away.

CHAPTER TWO

CLARA ALWAYS MULTITASKED. She had to—she couldn't manage the homes and lives of the over-privileged if she wasn't capable of sorting out babysitters, dog walkers and hedge trimmers whilst ordering a cordon bleu meal and cleaning a loo. Usually all at the same time. Driving was the perfect opportunity to gather her thoughts and make mental lists.

But not tonight. Her to do lists were slithering out of her mind, replaced by unwanted images of smiling eyes, a mobile mouth and a firmly confident manner.

Her own personal kryptonite.

Luckily this was probably the last she'd see of him. He would be on the early train to London each morning, return to Hopeford long after she had finished for the night and it wasn't as if she personally cleaned the house anyway.

Besides, Polly would be home soon and he would return to whichever beach he had reluctantly pulled himself away from faster than Clara could change the sheets and vacuum the rug. Things would be safe and steady.

So she had felt a little awareness. A tingle. Possibly even a jolt. It was allowed—she was twenty-nine, for goodness' sake, and single, not a nun. It wasn't as if she had taken vows of chastity.

It just felt that way sometimes. Often.

She should enjoy the moment—and make sure it didn't happen again.

Pulling into her parents' driveway, Clara took a moment and sat still in the fading light. This was usually one of her favourite times, the calm after a full and busy day, the moment's peace before other ties, welcome, needed, unbreakable ties, tugged at her, anchoring her firmly.

The house lights were on, casting a welcoming glow, beckoning her in. She knew she would step into warmth, love, gorgeous aromas drifting out of the kitchen, gentle chatter—and yet she sat a minute longer, slewing off the day, the last hour, until she could sit no more and slid down out of the van onto the carefully weeded gravel.

Clara's parents lived in a traditional nineteen-thirties semi-detached house in what used to be the new part of town. Now the trees had matured, the houses weathered and the new town had become almost as desirable as the old with families adding attic conversions, shiny glass extensions and imposing garages. The Castleton house was small by comparison, still with the original leaded bay windows and a wooden oval front door.

It was ten years since Clara had occupied the small bedroom at the back but the house itself was reassuringly gloriously unchanged.

'Evening,' she called out, opening the front door and stepping into the hallway.

'In here,' her father called from the kitchen and, lured by the tantalising smell, she followed his voice—and her nose.

'Something smells good.' Clara dropped a fond kiss on her father's cheek before bending down to sneak a look inside the oven.

'Spiced chickpea and spinach pastries in filo pastry.'

'I'd have thought you'd had enough kneading during the day,' she teased.

'It relaxes me. Have you got the list?'

'Of course.' Clara produced a neatly printed out list from a file in the cavernous bag she rarely ventured anywhere without. She used her father's deli for her customers' food requests whenever possible. He wasn't the cheapest, although, she thought loyally, he was definitely the best, but not one person ever balked at the hefty bill topped up with Clara's own cut. The prestige of knowing it was all locally made and sourced was enough for most people although she knew many of them also shopped at the local discount supermarket whilst making sure her father's distinctive purple labels were at the front of their pantries and fridges.

Clara put the list down onto the one clear part of the counter and mock glared at her father. 'It would save us both a lot of time if you let me email it to you.'

'Email me,' he scoffed as he pulled a selection of dressed salads out of the cavernous fridge. 'I'll be up making bread at six. When do I have time to read emails? Hungry?'

'For your pastry? Always. I'll be back in a moment.' She shook her head at him. Clara was always nagging her father to get more high tech, to get a website, engage on social media. The delicatessen was doing well, more than well, but with just a little marketing spur she didn't see why it couldn't do better, expand into neighbouring towns. The problem was her father liked to do everything himself.

Pot, kettle, she thought with a grin as she tore herself away from the kitchen and walked into the main room of the house where the sitting and dining room had been knocked through to create one big family space.

A large oak table dominated the back and Clara felt the usual lift in her heart when she spotted a small dark head bowed over a half-completed gothic Lego castle. This was what made it all worthwhile: the long hours, the repetitive work, the nights in alone.

'Impressive,' she said. 'Good day, sweetie?'

The head lifted, revealing a large pair of dark brown eyes. 'Mummy! You're late again.'

And just like that the happiness became swirled with guilt even though the comment hadn't been accusatory. The matter-of-factness was worse. Summer didn't expect her to be on time: she hardly ever was.

'Sorry, Sunshine. How was school?'

'Fine.'

Of course it was; everything was fine. Unless it was awesome, the ultimate accolade.

'I'm just going to eat and then we'll head home. Have you finished your homework?'

'Of course,' her daughter replied with quiet dignity before breaking into a most undignified grin as Clara walked around the table and gathered her in close for a long moment. Summer was getting taller, her head close to Clara's shoulders, the baby plumpness replaced by sharp bones and long limbs, but she still gave the most satisfying cuddles. Clara breathed her daughter in, steadying herself with the familiar scent of shampoo, fresh air and sweetness before releasing her reluctantly.

'I'll be no more than ten minutes,' she promised. 'We might have time for a quick half-hour's TV. Your turn to choose. Okay?'

It was like being a child herself, sitting at the kitchen table with a plate full of her father's trial runs whilst he quietly measured, stirred and tasted and her mother bustled from one room to the other whilst relating a long and very involved story about a dimly remembered school friend of Clara's who was, evidently, getting married. According to her mother the entire single population of Hopeford was currently entering wedlock, leaving Clara as the sole spinster of the parish.

Clara knew her mother was proud of her—but she also knew she would give a great deal to see her married. Or dating.

Heck, her mother would probably be more relieved than shocked if she spent every Saturday night cruising the local nightspots for casual sex.

Not that there were any real local nightspots other than a couple of pubs and even if she wanted to indulge the pickings were slim. A grin curved her lips at the thought of strutting into her local and coming onto any of the regulars. They'd probably call her parents in concern that she'd been taken ill!

'Clara.' The insistence in her mother's voice was a definite sign that she had moved on from a discussion of Lucy Taylor's appalling taste in bridesmaids' dresses and wanted her attention.

'Sorry, Mum. Miles away.'

'I was just thinking, why not leave Summer here with us tonight so you can go out?' Clara repressed a sigh. It was as she had feared. All this talk of weddings had addled her mother's brain.

'Go out?'

'Your cousin is back home for a couple of weeks. I know she's planning to go to The Swan tonight. It would be lovely if you joined her.'

For just one moment Clara experienced a rare shock of envy. That had once been her plan, a job and a life away from the well-meaning but prying eyes of her hometown.

'I've got a lot of work to do—I've promised Summer

some time before bed but then I must spend a fun couple of hours with the timetables.' She attempted a smile. It wasn't that she minded working all hours but it didn't sound very glamorous.

'Come on, love,' her mother urged. 'You never get to go out. Just one drink.'

It would be so easy to give in. Put the computer away for the evening, go out and get all the gossip about her cousin Maddie's impossibly exciting life as a stylist on a popular reality show. But duty called. She had to remain firm.

She couldn't just drop everything for an unscheduled night out. No, it was absolutely impossible.

'I've been thinking.' Clara wound her hand around the half-pint glass, pointedly avoiding her cousin's eyes. 'Maybe it's time I should consider internet dating.'

Clara knew she was fairly stubborn. Unfortunately it was a trait she had inherited from her mother and passed down to her daughter. United they were a formidable team and when her dad had added his gentle voice to theirs she had been quite outgunned.

Clara had been sent out for fun whether she liked it or not.

And now she was out, she was beginning to wonder again whether her mother might be right about more than Clara's need for a night off.

'Internet dating?' Maddie squealed at a pitch that could cause serious discomfort to dogs. 'Any dating would be a good start. Isn't there anyone closer to home though? I have stories about internet disasters that would make your hair curl. I know you, one disaster and you'll give the whole thing up. And there will be a disaster.' She nodded sagely. 'There always is.'

'Nope. I went to school with, babysat for, employed or have been employed by every single man I know in a ten-mile radius without a single spark. And this way I can profile them first, make sure they're suitable.'

'*If* they tell you the truth,' Maddie said darkly. 'Don't contact anyone without clearing them with me first. I know the language they use.'

Clara laughed, trying to quell the unease Maddie's words conjured up. How would she know who to trust? It had been such a long time ago—and she'd got it horribly wrong then. It wasn't just her pride at stake now; there was Summer too. She'd messed up so badly with Summer's own father, any new man in their lives had to be perfect. Her daughter deserved the best. 'I promise, you get first approval.'

'Ooh, we could have a look now.' Maddie had pulled out her phone and was jabbing away at the screen. 'What are you looking for?'

'Sensible, hardworking with good values.' It didn't take Clara long to think. These things counted for far more than the tilt of a mouth or a warm glint in a pair of navy-blue eyes.

'Very exciting. Any speciality? I have accounts with Uniformly Single, Farmers for You, Country Ladies and Gents and Parents Need Love Too. We could see who is available locally! So, hot fireman, beefy farmer or a fabulous father?'

'They are not all real accounts.' Clara stared at Maddie's phone in disbelief. 'I thought you were happy with Olly.'

'I *am*, but he's an actor. First whiff of success and he'll be off. There's no harm in keeping my accounts open and having the occasional peep.'

'Isn't there anyone, you know, normal?' This was a

bad idea. What had she been thinking, mentioning it to Maddie? She'd meant to do some research first. Approach the whole thing in a sensible businesslike way.

'I still think you're better off warming up on someone you know.' Maddie was scanning around the pub hopefully like a hound on the scent. 'Get back in the saddle before you start galloping. There must be *someone* in here you can practise on.'

It was only Tuesday but that hadn't stopped a constant stream of people popping in for a quick drink or settling in for a longer session. The cousins had bagged a prime position at the corner of the L-shaped room and from her comfortable armchair Clara could see all the comings and goings in the friendly local.

She was out so rarely she felt vaguely guilty, as if she were seventeen again, illicitly consuming half a lager shandy and hoping that the barman didn't ask for ID, jumping every time the door opened in case her parents came in to march her home.

Although these days they would buy her another and beg her to stay.

'Hang on.' Maddie froze as she zoomed in on some unsuspecting prey like the expert hunter she was. 'He looks promising. How about him?'

Clara's chest tightened, an unsettling feeling quivering in her stomach as she saw just who Maddie was staring at. This wasn't who she had been looking for all evening, was it? Wasn't the reason her heart had jumped in painful anticipation each time the door opened?

Stop it, she told herself fiercely.

Raff Rafferty was standing at the entrance looking around the pub. As his eyes swept over Clara they stopped and he smiled slightly, raising one tanned hand in greeting. How embarrassing; he'd seen her staring.

Hoping she wasn't blushing too much, Clara snapped her eyes away, regarding her empty glass with every appearance of absorbed interest.

'You *know* him?' Maddie was still staring in undisguised admiration at Raff. 'Things *have* changed around here, and for the better. You've kept him quiet.'

'I don't actually know him.' Clara was aware how unnaturally defensive she sounded and tried to rein it back in. 'He's new—to town, I mean, but he's not staying for long. He's completely unsuitable.'

'Hot and temporary, sounds perfect for a trial run to me. Sure you're not tempted?'

Clara couldn't quite meet Maddie's enquiring gaze. 'Quite sure. His sister is a client of mine.'

'Oh,' Maddie sighed. 'What a shame he's not a new permanent resident. We could do with some eye candy in this town. Hang on.' Maddie perked up. 'He's coming this way!'

Clara's stomach gave that peculiar twist again. It was a shame that stomachs couldn't qualify for the Olympics because by the feel of the double somersault hers was doing right now she was pretty sure she would score highly on rhythmic gymnastics.

'Clara Castleton.' It was said politely but there was a gleam in Raff Rafferty's eye that unnerved her. As if he was laughing at her.

She looked up as coolly as she could. 'The quiche didn't suit after all?'

'It was delicious,' he assured her. 'But I fancied a drink. Can I get you two ladies a top up?'

Raff turned the full beam of his blue eyes onto Maddie and Clara felt her jaw clench as her cousin beamed back. 'That would be lovely,' Maddie said as Clara blurted out, 'Thank you but we are fine.'

'Come and join us,' Maddie invited, shooting a conspiratorial look at Clara.

'I'm sure Mr Rafferty has somewhere he would rather be.' It was Clara's turn to be signalling her cousin with a meaningful look but Maddie wasn't being very receptive.

'That's a shame.' Maddie smiled up at Raff. 'Do you?'

'I don't think so.' Raff was looking amused. 'I don't have any friends here so I'd love to join you, thanks. I'm Raff.'

'Maddie.' She was positively purring. 'Raff Rafferty, that's an unusual combination. Your parents liked it so much they used it twice?'

He grinned, annoyingly at his ease. 'I wish. No, my mother was into Greek mythology so when she knew she was having twins she decided to name us after the heavenly twins, Castor and Pollux. My sister escaped with Polly. I wasn't so lucky.'

'I like it,' Maddie said. 'It's unusual.'

Clara caught Raff's eye in a moment of shared amusement, an intoxicating warmth spreading through her at the laughter in his eyes.

'You wouldn't like being called Sugar all the time,' Raff assured her cousin. 'After one week at prep school and five fights I changed it to Raff. Now only my grandparents use my real name.'

'It could have been worse.' Clara had been thinking. 'If she'd known you were a boy and a girl you might have been Apollo and Artemis.'

'Good God, literally!' Raff looked horrified. 'I will never despise my name again. What a lucky escape I had. For that I absolutely must get you a drink. What are you drinking?'

Clara opened her mouth fully intending to say no again and more firmly this time, but something extraordinary happened and the words in her head changed as soon as they left her mouth. 'Thank you,' she said. 'I'm drinking the local pale ale.'

Raff hadn't intended to leave the house tonight. It had taken him over two days to get back to England and once the plane had touched down at Gatwick he had headed straight to Hopeford like a homing pigeon aiming for a new world record.

He'd hoped that the key to finding Polly would be right here in the surprisingly shapely form of Clara Castleton or hidden somewhere in Polly's house—and he was going to find it whatever it took.

Only it turned out that being mad with his twin wasn't enough; he simply couldn't invade her privacy. One step into her study and he had frozen. He might not like it but Polly was entitled to her secrets.

For a long time they had only really had each other. Now they didn't even have that. The moment she'd started blaming Raff for their grandfather's blatant favouritism it had all fallen apart and everything Raff did made it worse. Even when he'd finally left, finally had the courage to follow his own path, he couldn't make it right.

He didn't know *how* to repair the damage—if it was even repairable. But whatever she thought, she could rely on him. He'd find out where she was, what was wrong and he'd fix it. Fix them.

So here he was. She'd asked him—told him—to come home and he had. But now what?

His mood had turned dark, exhaustion and frustration making rest impossible, introspection unbearable. Five minutes of television channel hopping later and Raff had had enough. It was time to go and check out the ridiculously quaint town his sister had bequeathed him.

Otherwise he was going to end up having a conversation with the cat. Mr Simpkins knew more than he was letting on; he was sure of it.

It didn't take Raff long to explore. Hopeford defined sleepy small town, was the epitome of privileged. The narrow streets closed in around him, making it hard to breathe. This rarefied atmosphere was exactly what he had been running from the last four years.

He'd breathed a sigh of relief at the familiar sign hanging outside a half-timbered building. A pub, a chance to get his head together, regroup. Four years of changing places, of new jobs, new challenges all had one thing in common. A local watering hole. A place to find out the lie of the land, find some compatible companionship and quench his thirst. The Swan was a little older, a lot cleaner and a great deal safer than his last local but he didn't hold that against the place.

Especially when he walked in and clapped eyes on Clara Castleton.

It had taken a moment or two to recognise her. Sure there was the same feline tilt to her long-lashed eyes, the same high cheekbones but that was where the similarity ended. This version had let her hair down, metaphorically as well as physically, the strawberry-blonde length allowed to fall in a soft half-ponytail rather than ruthlessly pulled back.

Even more disturbingly the lush full mouth was curved in a generous smile.

But none of that mattered. Clara was a means to an end, that was all. Mr Simpkins might not be ready to talk but a friendly night in the pub and he might have Clara telling him anything he needed to know. She must know more than she was letting on—she ran every aspect of Polly's life.

'Thank you for the drink…' oh, no, prim was back '…but I really need to be going.'

Raff glanced at his battered old watch. His grandfather had given him a Breitling for his twenty-first but he preferred the cheap leather-strapped watch he had bought first trip out. Bought with money earned by his own sweat, not by family connections.

'It's still early. Are you sure you don't want to stay a bit longer?'

'It's a work night,' she reminded him. Raff had been doing his best to forget. Tomorrow he was going to have to try and dig up something smart, get up ridiculously early and join all the other pack rats on an overpriced, overcrowded train. No matter he hadn't made this exact journey before. He knew the drill.

The only surprise was whether his particular carriage would be overheated or freezing cold. Unlike Goldilocks, Raff was under no illusions that it would be just right.

'Yes, it is,' he agreed. 'Unless you tell me where Polly is and save me from a day in the office tomorrow?'

She sighed as she got to her feet, gathering her bag and coat in her arms. 'I already told you…'

He'd blown it. He was too tired to play the game properly. He made one last-ditch attempt. 'I'm sorry. Let me walk you home.'

'Why? So you can interrogate me some more?' She shook her head, the red-gold tendrils trembling against her neck.

'No.' Well, only partly. 'It's good manners.' In some of the places Raff had lived you always saw the girl home. Even if it was the tent next to yours.

She shot him an amused glance. 'I think I'll be okay.'

'I won't,' he assured her. 'I'll lie awake all night worrying I failed in my chivalric duty. And I'll have to go to work tomorrow all red-eyed and pale from worry and they will all think I've been out carousing all night. Which will be most unfair as it's barely nine p.m.'

'I don't live far.' But it wasn't a no and she didn't complain as he drained his drink and followed her out, noting the blush that crept over her cheeks as she said goodbye to her cousin, who pulled her close for a hug and to whisper something in her ear.

'Where to?' he asked as he fell into step beside her. She walked just as he'd thought she would, purposeful, long strides in her sensible low-heeled boots.

'I live above the office.'

That wasn't a surprise. 'All work and no play...' he teased. It wasn't meant with any malice but to his surprise she stopped and turned, the light from the lamp post highlighting the colour in her cheeks.

'Why do people think it's a bad thing to concentrate on work?' she asked. Raff didn't reply; he could tell the question wasn't really aimed at him. 'So I work hard. I want to provide stability for my daughter. Is that such a bad thing?'

Daughter?

'I didn't know you were married,' he said and wanted to recall the words as soon as he said them. This wasn't the nineteen fifties and she wasn't wearing a ring.

'I'm not,' she said coldly and resumed walking even faster than before.

Way to go, Raff, nice building of rapport, he thought wryly. *You'll get Polly's address out of her in no time.*

He cast about for a safer topic. 'How old is she? Your daughter?'

'Ten,' she said shortly but he could feel her soften, see her shoulders relax slightly. 'Her name's Summer.'

'Pretty.'

'I was in a bit of a hippy stage at the time,' she confessed. 'Summer says she's glad she was born then because I'd probably call her something sensible and boring now. But it suits her.'

'Does she live with you?'

'I know the flat's not ideal for a child,' she said. Why did she assume every question was a criticism? 'But there's a garden at my parents' and she spends a lot of time there.'

'I spent a lot of time with my grandparents too.' During the school holidays it had been the only home he'd known.

'Polly said they brought you up.' It was a simple statement; there was no curiosity or prying behind it but it shocked him all the same. Polly was confiding in Clara, then. No wonder she hadn't put the welcome mat out for him.

What else had his twin said?

'Do you see a lot of Polly?' The question was abrupt and he tried to soften it. 'We're not really in touch any more. I'm glad she has a friend here.'

'We're both busy but we catch up when we can.' It wasn't enough but he didn't know how to push the issue without frightening her off.

And at least Polly had someone looking out for her. He tried again. 'If you care for all your clients the way you look after Polly, no wonder you're so busy.'

'Not all of them. Some just want cleaners and gardeners, others like to outsource all their home maintenance. Or I can provide babysitters, a shopping service, interior designers. Often it's just putting people in touch with the right services.'

'And taking a cut?'

Clara smiled. 'Of course. But some people need me

on call twenty-four seven, to pick up dry-cleaning, pick the kids up from school, buy last-minute gifts. Whatever they need I supply.'

She sounded so calm, so utterly in control and yet she was what? Late-twenties? A couple of years younger than Raff.

'Impressive.' He meant it.

'Not really.' She sounded a little less sure. 'None of it was really planned.' She had slowed down, her step less decisive, nervously twisting the delicate silver bangle on her wrist round and round. 'I had Summer and I needed to work. Oh, I know my parents would have let us live there. They wanted me to go to university but I couldn't just offload my responsibilities onto them. There's a lot of incomers in Hopeford, busy commuters with no time and a lot of money. I started cleaning for them and things kind of snowballed.'

She made it sound so easy but Raff was in no doubt that building her business up from cleaning services to the slick operation she ran today had taken a lot of grit and determination.

'I'd love Summer to have a proper home.' She sounded a little wistful. 'A kitchen like Polly's and a huge garden. But living above the office is practical—and it's ours. It was a better investment than a house at this stage in our lives.'

Investment, plans. It was like an alternative universe to a man who lived out of a kitbag and changed countries more frequently than he had his hair cut.

'This is me.' Clara had come to a stop outside the leaded bow window. She stood at the door calm, composed. 'Do you think you can find your way back or do I need to walk *you* home now?'

Her face was unreadable and there was no hint of flirtatiousness in her manner. Was she trying to be funny or was she completely serious? Raff couldn't figure her out at all. 'I have an excellent sense of direction,' he assured her. 'So…'

'Goodnight, then.' She offered him her hand, a quaintly old-fashioned gesture. Their eyes met, held; Raff could see uncertainty in her gaze as she stood there for one long second before she abruptly stepped back and turned, hands fumbling with her keys.

And she was gone without even one last backward glance.

Raff let out a long breath, an unexpected stab of disappointment shocking him. *Fool,* he told himself. *You're not here to flirt and, even if you had the time or inclination, since when were ice maidens your style?* He was tired, that was all, the jet lag clouding his judgement.

He had a job to do: find Polly, get her home, return to his real life. Nothing and no one, especially not the possessor of a pair of upwardly tilted green eyes, was going to get in his way.

CHAPTER THREE

WHAT WAS THAT?

Clara looked up as the front door creaked, but it was only someone walking by. Old buildings and narrow pavements equalled many creaks and bangs. It was a good thing she wasn't a nervous type.

Nor was she usually the door-watching type.

But it was getting to be a habit.

First at the pub, now today. And yesterday.

She was pathetic.

Especially as she knew only too well that Raff Rafferty hadn't even set foot in Hopeford in the last three days. He had, she guessed, boarded the train to London on Wednesday morning along with all the rest of the commuters but, according to Sue, the woman who usually cleaned the Rafferty house, he hadn't been back since. His bed was unrumpled, no dishes had been used, no laundry left. Either he was extraordinarily tidy, so tidy even Sue's legendary forensic skills couldn't find any trace of him, or he was staying in London.

This was all Maddie's fault. If she hadn't pulled her aside, told her to invite him in for coffee. 'It's not always a euphemism,' she'd said, mischief glinting in those green eyes so like Clara's own. Only brighter, livelier, flirtier. 'Not unless you want it to be...'

Of course she didn't. And coffee at that time of night was irresponsible anyway—inviting someone in for a cup of peppermint tea was probably never misconstrued. She could have done that. But did she want to? Want that tall, confident man in her flat? Even for one innocent cup of hot herbal beverage?

Because there was one moment when he had looked down at her and her breath had caught in her throat, every nerve end pulsing with an anticipation she hadn't felt in years. If she had stepped forward rather than backwards, if he had put his hands on her shoulders, angled his mouth down to hers, what would she have done?

Clara slumped forward. This all proved that she had taken the whole not-dating, stability-for-Summer thing just a tiny bit too far. If she had allowed her mother to set her up, just occasionally, for dinner and drinks with one of the many eligible men she had suggested over the years, then one measly hour in the pub, one small drink, wouldn't have thrown her so decidedly off kilter.

Raff Rafferty had been a tiny drop of water after a long drought. It didn't mean he was the *right* kind of water but just one taste had reminded her of what she was missing. What it felt like to have an attractive man's attention focused solely on her.

Even if he did have an ulterior motive that had nothing to do with Clara herself.

'That's a fearsome frown. Planning to murder someone?'

After all that waiting she hadn't even heard the door open.

She hoped he hadn't seen her jump, that the heat in her cheeks wasn't visible. 'I exact a high penalty for unpaid bills.'

Clara had been hoping that three days' absence had

exaggerated Raff's attractiveness. They hadn't. He was just as tall, as broad as she remembered but the weary air she had glimpsed last time was unequivocal. He looked as if he hadn't slept for a week.

Dark circles shadowed his eyes, unfairly emphasising the navy blue, his face was pale under the deep tan, the well-cut shirt was wrinkled.

'I need a favour.' He didn't even crack a smile. 'Just how full a service do you offer?'

Clara gaped at him. 'I beg your pardon?'

'I asked...' he spoke slowly, clearly, enunciating every word '...how full a service you offer. I need a girlfriend and I need one now. Can you supply me with one, or not?'

If he hadn't been so tired... If he hadn't been quite so desperate, then Raff might have phrased his request slightly differently. As it was it took a while for the outrage on Clara's face to penetrate the dense fog suffocating what was left of his brain.

'You're not the first person to ask me for extra services,' she said finally, contempt dripping through her words. 'I admit, though, you have surprised me. I would have thought you were quite capable of hiring your own special help.'

Something was wrong, Raff could dimly tell, but he fixed on the positive.

'So you can help me?'

'Normally it's the bored wives that ask for something extra. Someone to help *clean out the guttering, trim the borders.*' She put a peculiar emphasis on the last few words. 'I do like to help them when I can. I usually send Dave round. He might be seventy-three but he's steady up a ladder. They don't ask again.'

Raff tried to sort out her meaning from her words. He was quite clearly missing something. 'Do the gutters need doing?' he asked. 'Surely that's your preserve, not mine. Do what you think best. Look, it's been a long day, a long week. Can you help me or not?'

She looked at him levelly but to his astonishment there was a cold anger in her eyes. 'Not. This is a concierge service not an escort service. Now please leave. Now.'

'What?' Raff shook his head in disbelief as her words sank in. 'I don't want… I didn't mean. For crying out loud, Clara, what kind of man do you think I am?'

'I don't know,' she retorted, eyes hot with fury now. 'The kind of man who walks away from his family, the kind of man who doesn't have to work for anything worth having! The kind of man who wants to rent a girlfriend—'

'Yes! A girlfriend. Not an escort or a call girl or whatever your dirty little brain has conjured up.' Now his anger was matching hers, the righteous fury waking him up. 'If I was looking for someone to sleep with I could find them, don't worry your pretty little head about that, but that's not what I'm looking for. I need someone to come to a few functions with me, to gaze lovingly into my eyes and to convince an autocratic old man that I might just settle down with her. Now, is that something you can help me with?'

If he thought his words might make her feel guilty, get her to back down, then he rapidly realised he was wrong. She uncoiled herself from her seat, rising to her feet to look up into his face, her eyes fixed on his, full of righteous anger.

'This is about fooling your grandfather? Why? So he doesn't cut you off? I have had it up to here with poor little rich boys who live their lives according to who holds the purse strings. I wouldn't help you if I had a hundred suitable girls working for me. Now please leave.'

Raff choked back a bitter laugh. 'I don't have to justify myself to you, Miss Castleton, but for your information my grandfather is ill. He's in the hospital and I am under strict orders not to upset him. So I either start dating one of the unfortunate women on the shortlist he drew up for me, fake a relationship or be responsible for yet another dangerous rise in blood pressure.'

He smiled over at her, sweet and dangerous. 'Tell me, Miss Know-it-all, which do you recommend?'

'A shortlist?'

That had stopped Miss Judgemental in her tracks.

Raff didn't want to let go of the anger and frustration, didn't want to try and tease a responsive grin from that pursed-up mouth, coax a glint out of those hard emerald eyes.

Especially as her words had cut a little deeper than they should. No virtual stranger should have the power to penetrate beneath the shield he so carefully erected yet her words had been like well-aimed arrows piercing straight into his Achilles heel.

Whether it was the lack of sleep, the taut tension in the room or the craziness of the situation, he didn't know but, despite his best intentions, a slow smile crept over his face.

'Do you want to see it?'

Clara's eyes widened. 'You have it with you?'

'I needed something to read on the train. Here.' He pulled the sheaf of papers out of his coat pocket and held them out. 'Names, pedigrees, biographies and photographs.'

She made no attempt to take them. 'Thorough.'

'He means business,' Raff agreed, letting the papers fall down onto the desk with an audible thump. It felt as if he had put down a heavy burden. 'Now do you understand?'

She still wasn't giving an inch. 'Couldn't you just talk to him?'

Raff laughed. 'No one *just talks* to Charles Rafferty. We all tug our forelock and scuttle away to do his bidding. Or run away. Both Polly and I took that route.'

He sighed and picked the papers up again, shuffling them. 'I owe you an apology. It doesn't matter even if you do know where Polly is...' she opened her mouth to interject and he held up his hand '...but I'm sure you don't. She's covered her traces well and I don't blame her.'

The only person he could blame right now was himself. They were so estranged she couldn't, wouldn't confide in him.

Concern was etched onto Clara's face. 'Is she okay?'

Raff shook his head. 'I doubt it. It turns out that great profits and great PR aren't enough. My grandfather showed his gratitude for an another excellent year's trading by telling Polly he was never going to make her CEO, and he is going to sign the company over to me.'

'Ouch.'

Clara sank back into her seat, a sign the battle was over. Thank goodness. Raff had been through enough emotional wars in the last few days. He leant against her desk, grateful for the support. 'That was just the start of it.' Raff ran a hand through his hair. Damn, he was tired. What a ridiculous mess. 'We owe him a lot, Polly and me. It's hard to stand up to him. But this was so wrong I had to say something.' His mouth twisted as he pictured the scene. 'I managed to stay calm but he got completely worked up and ended up collapsing in the most dramatic fashion.'

Raff was aware that he was making light of the situation, but the moment his grandfather had clutched his chest and collapsed was branded in his mind. 'I thought we'd lost him.'

Clara reached a tentative hand across the desk, then pulled it back, seemingly unsure how to react. 'Is he okay?'

'Angina. Apparently he's kept that a secret along with his plans. He's to be kept quiet and not allowed to get worked up, which is a little like telling a baby not to cry. And he is taking full advantage of the situation.' Despite himself Raff grinned. He had to admire his grandfather's sheer bloody-mindedness.

'As soon as I walked through the hospital-room door today he handed me this list.' He held up his hands. 'I know I should have told him the truth right then but seeing as the last time I upset him he collapsed, I didn't. I admit I panicked—next thing I knew I was telling him I had a girlfriend already, it was pretty serious and I was agreeing to bring her along to meet him on Sunday. Two days isn't a long time to find a convincing fake girlfriend, you know.'

Clara leant back in her chair and regarded him solemnly but Raff could swear those cat's eyes of hers were sparkling. 'You seem to be in somewhat of a predicament.'

'I am.' He nodded, trying his best to look downcast as hope shot through him. He needed someone cool, someone professional, someone who understood the rules. She would be perfect, if he could just make her see it.

'I don't understand why you lied in the first place. A

few dates isn't going to kill you, is it?' She was looking stern again.

Raff sighed. It was so hard to explain without sounding like an arrogant idiot. 'I have no intention of sticking around and raising expectations would be unfair.'

'Presumptuous.'

'Hardly.' He laughed but there was little humour in it. 'These women aren't the sort to get carried away, at least not where their futures are concerned. The Rafferty name and fortune is old enough and big enough to put me on several "most eligible bachelor" lists. Why do you think I stay out of the country?'

'Is marriage and a family really so terrible?' For a moment Raff thought he saw sadness shimmering in her face but one blink and it was gone, replaced by her usual cool professionalism.

'No,' he admitted. 'But not for me, not yet. There's a lot I need to do before I'm ready for that kind of commitment.'

If he ever was. He'd seen firsthand just what marriage could do. He still didn't know what was worse: his grandmother staying put out of martyred duty or his mother fleeing as soon as things got tough. Either way it had been hard for Polly and him.

Not that any of his school friends had fared much better. Outside gravy adverts, he still wasn't entirely sure that happy families existed.

'Look, I appreciate that I approached this all wrong but I could really use your help.'

She shook her head. 'It doesn't feel right.'

'Clara, please.' He wasn't too proud to beg. 'You would be perfect: you own your own business, know Polly. My grandfather will adore you.'

'Me!' Was that panic on her face? But there was something else too. She was trying to hide it but she was intrigued.

Raff pressed the point home. 'Look, I'll pay you by the day, even if I only need you for a couple of hours, and I'll owe you. There must be something I can do for you. Don't you need an eligible date at all? Wedding, christening, bar mitzvah?'

'My diary's empty.' But her lush mouth was tilted up into a smile. 'Socially at least.'

'Even better,' he said promptly. 'I'm promising you fine dining, glamorous parties and a clothes allowance. Think of me as a particularly masculine fairy godfather whisking you away to the ball.'

'I can't just drop everything.' But, oh, she looked tempted. 'I have a business, a daughter. What's she supposed to do whilst I'm out gallivanting with you?'

'Gallivanting and drumming up business,' Raff said slyly. Bullseye. Temptation was giving way to interest. 'Think of the contacts you'll make.'

'Contacts in London,' she demurred.

'With your talents it wouldn't matter if they lived in Antarctica,' he assured her. 'You'll be soothing out the wrinkles in half of London's lives in no time. And it won't be for long. I'm hoping to get everything sorted out within a month, six weeks tops. I'm sure your parents won't mind babysitting.'

'No.' She looked down at her computer screen, shielding her expression from him. 'I don't know, Raff. I'd have to call in a lot of favours, for work and Summer. I need to think about it.'

'I'll pay you double your daily rate and cover all costs. And if we're successful a bonus. Ten thousand pounds.'

'That's the second time this week you've offered

me ten thousand pounds.' Clara smiled sweetly at him. 'Burning a hole in your pocket?'

Ten thousand pounds. Small change to someone like Raff Rafferty but not to her. Add the daily double rate and this job looked as if it could be pretty lucrative.

A much-needed cash injection. Sure, things were ticking along nicely, turnover was healthy. But so were her outgoings. She chose her staff carefully and paid them well, used the best products, made sure she had people on call at all hours. She had a brilliant reputation but maintaining it cost money. It made it hard to save enough to expand and she was wary of borrowing.

If this extra job lasted six weeks she could make fifteen thousand pounds more than she had budgeted for. Enough for recruitment and advertising in a wider area, another small van. Maybe she could even engage a part-time PA for the office? She handled so many of the emails and calls whilst she was out and about. Keeping the office open and staffed in business hours would be fantastic.

It would be added security. For her and for her daughter.

But it would mean spending those next six weeks with Raff Rafferty. A man who unnerved her, flustered her. Could she handle it?

He was still perched on her desk, affecting nonchalance, but the tense set of his shoulders was a giveaway. He wasn't as relaxed as he liked to make out. He needed her.

Automatically she tapped at her keyboard, lighting up the dormant screen and clicking onto her emails, the very act beginning to calm her taut nerves. The long list of unread emails in bold might daunt some people but she found them soothing, purposeful and she scanned through the subject lines looking for an answer, a reason to turn him down.

Or an excuse to say yes.

Her inbox was the usual mixture of confirmations, enquiries, queries, staff correspondence and sales, nothing meaty, nothing distracting at all. She was about to close it down when a name caught her eye. Pressure filled her chest, making it hard to breathe, and for one long moment everything, the room, Raff Rafferty, her work disappeared.

An email from Byron.

Clara blinked, unsure whether she was seeing things or if the email was actually there. Her hand hovered over her mouse, unable to click as dizzying possibilities filled her mind. *He was coming over, he wanted to see Summer, to be involved.*

Her daughter wanted for nothing, except for an interested, loving father. Could that be about to change? This was the first time he had contacted her in ten years—that had to be a good sign, right?

'Clara, are you okay? If you don't want to do it that's fine. I'll call in a favour or two. I'd have preferred to keep things professional, that's all.'

'What?' With difficulty Clara fought her way past all the possibilities and emotions swirling dizzily around her brain. 'Sorry, I just need to read this. I'll be with you in a second.'

She noticed detachedly that her hand was shaking as she clicked on the email, the words were dancing in front of her eyes, making no sense at all. She blinked again, forcing herself to concentrate.

Dear Miss Castleton...

The opening line made her reel back, shocked by its formality, but, grimly determined, she read on.

Both Mr Byron Drewe and Mr Archibald Drewe will be visiting London the first week in May and would like to know if it is convenient for you to meet with them to discuss your daughter's future. Her presence is not required at the meeting.

Please send me any dates and times that week that would be convenient for you to meet and I will let you know the final arrangements and venue nearer the time. Any expenses you incur will of course be covered. Please provide the relevant receipts.

On behalf Mr Drewe Jr

Her first communication in years—and it was from Byron's secretary.

Her head was suddenly clear, the dizziness and anticipation replaced with hotly righteous anger. How dared they? How dared they dismiss Summer, summon Clara as if she were a servant? How dared they offer to pay her expenses—as long as she provided receipts like an untrustworthy employee?

Although Byron's father had always thought she was a gold-digging good-time girl, she had just naively hoped Byron believed in her, believed in their daughter. Despite everything.

Byron had spent so much time stringing her along, promising her they would be a family, but he hadn't even had the guts to tell his father about the baby. And once his father found out that was the end.

It was a straight choice: Clara and Summer or his family fortune. Turned out it was no choice at all.

Even then he had lied, promised he'd find a way, that

he loved her, loved Summer. Her heart twisted painfully. He had just wanted her to leave quietly, to not make a scene.

Clara's eyes locked onto the photo that sat on her otherwise clutter-free desk and the anger left just as suddenly as it had arrived. Dark hair, dark eyes, just like her father. Clara's feelings didn't matter here; Byron's behaviour didn't either. Summer was the one who counted and this was the first communication she had had from her daughter's father in years. He wanted to meet. Maybe he wanted to be involved.

Or maybe not. But she had to try. If only she didn't have to do it all alone. Of course her parents would come with her if she asked, but she didn't trust them not to threaten to castrate Byron with the butter knife—or actually do it. Not that he didn't deserve it but it wasn't quite the reconciliation she was hoping for.

Her parents were amazing. Supportive and loving and endlessly giving with their time. Clara couldn't have managed without them. But every now and then she couldn't help but wonder what it would be like to be part of a couple, to have a co-parent. Someone who was there all the time to laugh with at the funny bits, to burst with pride at all the amazing things only a parent could truly understand. To help when things got a little bumpy.

It wasn't that she minded being both mother and father to her daughter, she just wished for Summer's sake that she didn't have to be.

Clara scrolled back to the top of the email and reread it intently. If it were just going to be Byron, then meeting him alone would have been difficult, probably emotional, but eminently doable. His father's presence changed everything. He was a hard, harsh man. Clara sagged. She tried so hard to be strong but she really didn't want to do this alone.

'Here, drink this.' A coffee slid across the desk, rich and dark. 'You look like you've had a shock.'

Clara reached out for the white mug, absurdly touched by the gesture. 'Thanks,' she said, blinking rapidly. *No, don't you dare cry,* she told herself fiercely.

'I make a good listener, you know.' He was back leaning against her desk, cradling a mug of his own, concern in his eyes. 'Besides, you know a lot of my family secrets.'

Clara opened her mouth, a polite rebuff on the tip of her tongue, but closed it as a thought hit her.

Maybe she didn't have to be alone after all?

The memory of his earlier offer hung there tempting, intoxicating. He owed her a favour. Anything she wanted. What if she didn't have to face Byron and his father alone?

'I'll do it.' The words were sudden, abrupt, loud in the quiet office. 'If you guarantee me double time in office hours, treble at evenings and weekends, the bonus at the end of the six weeks and…' she swallowed but forced herself to look up, to meet his eyes '…and you will accompany me to one meeting. Agreed?'

It was Raff's turn to pause, the blue eyes regarding her quizzically, probing beneath her armour. 'Agreed,' he said finally.

Clara exhaled the breath she didn't even know she was holding. 'It's a deal.' She held out her hand. 'I'll see you on Sunday.'

His hand reached out to take hers, folding over it in a gesture that was far more like a caress than a handshake. 'Tomorrow. I'll pick you up at noon.'

'But…' Clara tried to withdraw her hand but it was

held fast in his cool grip '…I thought you needed a date to meet your grandfather on Sunday.'

He smiled, the devilry back in his eyes. 'I do, but we need to get to know each other first. You and I are going on a date.'

CHAPTER FOUR

It was becoming an annoying habit, somehow agreeing to the outrageous when she meant to refuse.

She'd felt sorry for him, fool that she was. She'd been lured in by a weary expression, candour and charm. A moment of personal weakness.

And yet there was a certain excitement about getting dressed up, about going somewhere other than The Swan. About going out with an undeniably attractive man.

Even if it wasn't a real date.

It was probably a good thing she had said yes. It was so long since she had been on any kind of date she was bound to be a little rusty, a little awkward. This was an opportunity to practise without any pesky expectations hanging over her.

And that was all this fizz in her veins was. It certainly had nothing to do with Raff Rafferty. It was about a pretty dress, a chance to wear her hair down, to put on a lipstick a little darker, a little redder than she wore for work. A chance for heels.

No, Clara decided, eying herself critically in the mirror, she didn't look too shabby. The vintage-style green tea dress was flattering and demure teamed with black patent Mary Janes and her hair was behaving for once, falling in a soft wave onto her shoulders.

She glanced at her watch. Five minutes. She wanted to be downstairs, sitting at her desk, working when he arrived. She might be all dressed up but this was work. Letting him upstairs, into her private space, was a step far too far.

And there could be no blurred lines.

She took a long look around the small, cosy sitting room. It wasn't the grandest of homes, the fanciest. But it was hers, hers and Summer's. Her sanctuary.

She'd bought it, paid for it, chosen the wallpaper, decorated it. Okay, there was a patch where it wasn't perfectly lined up but it was hers.

Raff would dominate the room, suck all the air out of the space.

Make it unsafe.

The urge to sink onto the overstuffed velvet sofa was almost overwhelming. To play hooky from work, from responsibilities, from this devil's pact. She could curl up with a large bar of chocolate and a Cary Grant film, block out the world for a few blissful hours. She pulled her phone out of her bag—one call and this whole crazy arrangement would be over before it had even begun.

Just one click. So easy.

Her finger moved to the contact list icon and hovered there.

Brrriiiing! The doorbell's loud chime echoed through the room, making her jump.

Panic caught in her throat, making breathing difficult for one long second. Clara put her hand to her stomach and took a deep breath, purposefully clearing her mind, filling her lungs, allowing herself a moment to calm.

This isn't real, she told herself. *This is work. This is my business. I'm happy to clean loos, I'll stock shelves, I even pick up dog dirt. I should be looking forward to a*

*few weeks of socialising instead. Any of my staff would
kill to swap with me.*

She could do this.

But a part of her would much rather be scrubbing
a room out from top to bottom, picture rail to skirting
boards, than spend any more time alone with Raff Rafferty.

And the other part of her was looking forward to it
just a little bit too much.

'Relax, this is supposed to be fun.' Raff threw an amused
look over at his passenger. Clara sat up ramrod straight,
clutching the seat as if it were her last hope. 'I'm a safe
driver.'

'In a very old car.'

'She's not old, she's vintage.' He patted the steering
wheel appreciatively. 'These Porsche 911s were *the* It
Car in their day.'

'In the middle of the last century.'

'She's not quite that old. This is a seventies' design
classic.' It was the only car Raff had ever owned. She
might be red, convertible and need a lot of loving maintenance but she was a link to his father, the only link
he had.

'The seventies,' Clara scoffed. 'The decade that taste
forgot.'

Raff grinned. 'Sit back, Clara. Enjoy it—the wind in
your hair—if you'd let me put the top down that is, the
green of the countryside flashing by. What's not to love?'

Clara was twisting the silver bangle she was wearing
round and round. 'A date, you said. I thought you meant
a drink in The Swan or, if you wanted to go crazy, a meal
at Le Maison Bleu. This isn't a date. This is kidnap.'

'We are supposed to have been together for a few

months. Mad about each other.' Her body got even more rigid if that was at all possible. Raff suppressed a smile. 'So, we need to create a relationship full of memories in just one day. Now we can do this the easy way and actually enjoy ourselves or we can endure a torturous afternoon full of monosyllables and long silences.' His mouth quirked. 'Now, if we were faking a marriage then the latter would be fine.'

Was that a smile? An infinitesimal relaxation of all those rigid muscles?

'What's your favourite colour?'

'My what?' That made her move. Her head swung round so fast he thought she might get whiplash.

'Your favourite colour?'

She shook her head. 'I don't even…why on earth do you want to know that?'

'I'll go first.' He leant back into the leather seat, enjoying the cold of the steering wheel under his hands, the purr of the engine. 'Okay, my favourite colour is sea blue, the sea on a perfect sunny day. Favourite food is a good old-fashioned roast dinner, which is the boarding school boy in me, I know, but there are times when just the thought of Yorkshire puddings keeps me going. I didn't think I was a cat or a dog person but after three days of Mr Simpkins I am definitely veering towards the canine. You?'

He sneaked a look over at his passenger. She was still gripping onto the seat but her knuckles were no longer white. 'If I'd known there was going to be a quiz I'd have prepared,' she said, but her voice was less frosty.

It took a few long moments before she spoke again. 'Okay, green, I think. Spring is my favourite season. I hate it when the trees are bare. I grew up with cats so I'll stick up for Mr Simpkins. What was the other one?

Food? It's not sophisticated but when I was travelling and eating all this amazing street food I craved cheese sandwiches. My dad's cheese sandwiches. Home-made bread, cheddar so mature it can't remember being young and his patented plum chutney.'

'Just a simple sandwich?'

'As simple as it gets in my house. Dad's a foodie.'

'You went travelling?' That was unexpected. Maybe they had something in common after all. 'I can't exactly visualise you with a backpack! How old were you?'

There was a long pause. 'Eighteen,' she said finally.

'Where did you go?' As Raff knew all too well, most people jumped at the opportunity to recount every second of their travels. It could be worse than listening to other people's dreams. Clara Castleton was obviously the exception; her silence was so chilly it was as if he'd asked her to recite *The Rime of the Ancient Mariner*. Backwards.

'Thailand to start with,' she said reluctantly after the pause got too long. 'Cambodia, Vietnam and then Bali and on to Australia.' She paused again. 'I was there for two years.'

Raff shook his head. 'When I was eighteen I could barely find my own way to university, let alone travel halfway across the world. Your parents must have been worried sick.'

She laughed, a dry hard laugh with no humour in it. 'I was so sure I was invincible I think I had them fooled too.'

Fooled? Interesting word.

'I planned for so long I don't think there was room to worry, really.' She wasn't really talking to him, he realised, more lost in the past. 'My grandfather was in the merchant navy and he had always told me all these stories of places he had been to. I wanted to see it all. Other kids have posters of pop stars on their wall, I had maps and routes and pictures of magical places I wanted to go to. I was babysitting at thirteen, running errands for neighbours and every penny went into my travel fund. I was going to start out in Asia then Australia, New Zealand, on to Japan then South America, finishing off with a Greyhound trip round the States.'

He could picture her. Intent, focused, planning on conquering the world. 'Did you get to go? Did you see all of those places?'

'No.' Her voice was colourless. 'I had Summer instead.'

'Hang on.' He turned and looked at her rigid profile. 'Did you have your daughter while you were away?'

'She was born in Australia.'

He whistled softly. 'That must have been tough. So you cut your adventures short, flew home and became the responsible, capable woman you are today.' He shook his head. 'Quite some achievement.'

He thought he was such a tough guy but his adventures were orderly by comparison. He always knew where he was going to sleep that evening even if it was in a sleeping bag in a shared tent; he had a ticket back arranged, plans for a month of surfing and partying organised. He even got a wage, for goodness' sake. Clara had taken off at an age most people were still figuring out the Tube and had spent three years travelling. Even a pregnancy and a baby hadn't slowed her down.

When she didn't answer he turned to look at her; she was looking out of the window but her body was slumped. It wasn't the posture of someone who had achieved something remarkable. It was more like despair.

'Are you going to tell me where we are going?' she

asked, straightening and turning to him with a polite smile.

The confidences were obviously at an end.

'I don't need to tell you,' he said as he smoothly turned the car through a pair of metal gates, the only break in a sea of barbed-wire fencing that ran along one side of the road screening off the fields beyond. 'We're here.'

'We're what?' Clara twisted in her seat and looked around her, horror on her face as she took in the barbed wire. 'You *are* kidnapping me. Where are we? What is this?'

'*This* is one of the premier activity sites in the country.' Raff flashed her a smile. 'I hope you like mud.'

'You want me to do what?'

Clara wasn't sure what was worse. She ticked the offending items off on a mental list. Lists usually were soothing, bringing order and meaning.

She wasn't sure anything could bring meaning to her current situation.

First, the mud. There was certainly a lot of it, all greeny-brown, glutinous and deep. Second, the outfit. All that time spent wondering what to wear, turned out she needed baggy camouflage trousers, desert boots that had been worn by who knew how many other smelly, sweaty, muddy feet and a shapeless T-shirt that was the exact colour of the mud. Yep, it all came back to mud.

Mud that she, Clara Castleton, was supposed to be trampling, running, heck, apparently she was supposed to be crawling in it. On her belly.

Which brought her to number three. Men. Smirking men. Okay, toned, built men, the kind that actually stretched out their T-shirts in all kinds of good ways, who filled out the baggy trousers with bulging thighs, who wore the mud on their faces with aplomb. Men who belonged here as she most definitely did not.

The most annoying of the men, 'Call me Spiral', as *if* that were really his name, began to repeat the instructions in the same loud bark. 'Run through that trough, climb that rope, go over that bridge, swing across the ravine, crawl under the net, slide…'

'I heard all of that the first two times.' Clara folded her arms and glared up at him, deliberately ignoring the fourth and most annoying thing of all: a palpably amused Raff Rafferty. 'I'm still not clear why.'

'Because I told you to,' Spiral said with no hint of irony. 'Now get your butt over to the starting line.'

'Come on, Clara.' Raff was openly grinning. 'This is supposed to be fun. Where's your sense of adventure?'

Back in Australia. Left behind with her backpack, her travel journals and her well-thumbed traveller's guide.

'*This* is your idea of a date?' She rounded on him. 'What's wrong with a walk, a picnic, doves and flowers?'

'Too obvious. Besides, I had the chance to try this place out and see if I want to hire it for a staff conference. I'm multitasking. I thought you'd approve,' he said with a self-righteous air that made Clara want to smack him—or tip him into the mud that suddenly looked a lot more tempting.

'This isn't just a lousy date, it's a cheap date?'

Raff leant in close, his breath sweet on her cheek. 'It's a fake date and you are on triple time. Enjoy it. Think about what a lovely story it makes.'

Clara gritted her teeth. 'One for the grandkids?'

'In our case one for my grandfather. Do you want to go first or shall I show you how it's done?'

Eying the long trail of ropes, platforms, nets and pits, Clara felt her stomach drop. This was going to be incredibly undignified. But there was no way she was going to look weak in front of him. 'I'll go.'

She refused to look back as she walked to the start line, painfully aware that all the conversation had stopped and every khaki-clad man was staring at her, lips curled with amusement. They were waiting for her to fail. To give up.

They were in for a surprise. She hoped.

'Come on,' Clara told herself fiercely as she stood at the rope marking the beginning and stared out at what looked like miles of hell. The trail started with a long, shallow trough that Clara was supposed to run through. Correction, wade through. The trough was filled with the ubiquitous mud and led to a cargo net that she was sure was higher than her house.

That was just the start.

Weekly Pilates might be good for her stress levels but it hadn't prepared her for this.

'On the count of three,' Spiral roared. 'One, two, three!'

Clara hesitated for less than a second and then, with a muttered curse, pushed herself forward, managing not to yell as she sank calf deep into the cold, gloopy mud.

'Faster,' Spiral yelled. 'Are you a man or a mouse?'

Answering him would have used up more oxygen than he was worth. Clara set her mouth mutinously and forged on. Too slow and she would prove the smirking men right, too fast and she knew she'd pitch face first into the mud. She set herself a steady trot, trying to ignore the cold, clamminess on her lower legs and the sucking noise as she pulled her leg out of the mud and put one hand onto the rope net, ready to pull herself up the impossible height.

Her eyes were focused on each obstacle; there was

no room in her mind for anything but the task. Spiral's encouraging shouts, the cheers of the other staff were just background noise. Clara was aware of nothing but the hammering of her heart, the pounding of the blood in her ears, the burn in her thighs and her arms as she pulled, swung, jumped, waded and crawled. She had no idea how long she had been there. Minutes? Hours?

Heck, it could have been days.

'Come on, Clara.' How on earth had Raff caught up with her? He was breathing hard, his hair damp with exertion, the dark blue eyes alight with life. She should be mad with him; she was absolutely filthy, totally exhausted, every muscle hurt and people kept yelling at her. And yet...

Adrenaline was pumping through her so fast she was almost weightless; the whole world had contracted to this place, this task. She was alive. Really, truly alive.

She reached out for the rope swing, and missed. Immediately Raff was there, one arm steadying her as she leant further forward off the narrow wooden platform, reaching out into thin air.

'Got it!' Giddy with triumph, she grabbed the rope and pulled it back towards her. Putting both hands firmly on it, she wrapped one leg around it and tried to jump on it, slithering back down to the platform as she missed. 'Darn it!'

'Here, let me.'

Clara wanted to tell him no, that she had this, but he was too quick, steadying the rope and, as she jumped again, giving her a quick push up. A jolt of electricity ran through her as his hand pressed against her back but before she could react he had pushed and she was off, swinging through the air.

Her limbs were trembling with the exertion as she

reached the last obstacle, the crawl net. To conquer it successfully she had to lie down, fully face down, in the mud and wiggle her way under ten metres of tight net.

She took a deep breath, the oxygen a welcome tonic to her tired, gasping lungs, and flung herself down into the oozing depths, pushing herself under the net and wiggling through the endless claustrophobic dark, wet mud until she reached the final rope. Once her head was through she gulped in welcome, blessed, clean air before painfully pulling the rest of her out. She lay there collapsed in the mud for five seconds, too exhausted to try and get to her feet.

The mud didn't seem so bad any more. She couldn't tell where it ended and she began. She had turned into some kind of swamp monster.

'That was a very good try.' Spiral's loud tones intruded on the muddy peace and Clara forced herself to pull onto her knees. 'Well done, Clara.'

A glow of pride warmed her. 'Thanks,' she said, drawing her hand across her face, realising too late that rather than wipe the mud off she was adding to it. Spiral held out one meaty hand and effortlessly pulled her to her feet, wrapping a blanket—khaki, of course, she noted—around her shoulders and, grabbing a mug from a plastic picnic table, pressed it into her hands.

Tea. Milky, sugary, the opposite of how she usually liked it. It was utterly delicious.

'You survived.' Raff had eschewed his blanket but was cradling his tea just as eagerly as she was. 'What did you think?'

'That was…' filthy, hard, undignified, unexpected '…exhilarating.'

He broke into an open grin. 'Wasn't it? Do you think

my staff will enjoy it? I thought that it could be the performance award this year. Followed by dinner, of course!'

'That sounds good.' As the adrenaline wore off Clara was increasingly aware of how cold she was; she suppressed a shiver. 'I hope you're going to let them get changed before dinner.'

'I'm kind like that.' He eyed her critically. 'Talking of which, you look freezing. The showers are back in the changing room. Go, warm up, get changed and then I owe you lunch, anything you want.'

Hot water, clean clothes, food. They all sounded impossibly, improbably good. 'You do owe me,' she agreed, putting the mug back onto the table before taking a few steps towards the low stone building where nirvana waited. She paused, impelled by a sudden need to say something, something unexpected.

'Raff,' she said. 'I had fun. Thank you.'

It was the last thing he had expected her to say. Standing there completely covered in mud, the baggy trousers plastered to her legs, the filthy T-shirt clinging to every curve. Raff had expected sulking or yelling, even downright refusal. He didn't expect her to thank him.

He'd known the challenge would shake her up, had secretly enjoyed the thought of seeing prim and judgemental Clara Castleton pushed so far out of her comfort zone—turned out the joke was on him.

'I'm glad,' he said, aware of how inadequate his response was. 'I thought you'd enjoy it.'

Clara smiled. A proper, full-on beam that lightened her eyes to a perfect sea green, emphasised the curve of her cheeks, the fullness of her mouth. She was dirty, bedraggled and utterly mesmerising. The breath left his body with an audible whoosh.

'Liar,' she said. 'You thought I'd hate it. And you were this close...' she held up her hand, her forefinger and thumb just a centimetre apart '...this close to being right.'

'Yes.' The blood was hammering through his veins, loud, insistent. All he could focus on was her wide mouth, the lines of her body revealed so unexpectedly by her wet clothes. What would it be like to take that step forward? To pull her close? To taste her?

Dangerous.

The word flashed through his mind. It would be dangerous; she would be dangerous. Workaholic single mothers were not his style no matter how enticing their smile. Women like Clara wanted commitment, even if they didn't admit it.

They played by different rules and he needed to remember it—no matter how tempted he was to forget.

CHAPTER FIVE

'THAT WASN'T TOO BAD.' Clara's smile and tone were more than a little forced. At least she was trying.

Which was more than his grandfather had.

'It was terrible.' Raff shook his head, unsure who he was more cross with: his grandfather for being so very rude, or himself for expecting anything different.

He *had* expected his grandfather to be terse and angry with him; it would take more than a suspected heart attack and a week in hospital for Charles Rafferty to get over any kind of insubordination even from his favourite grandson. It was the way he had spoken to Clara that rankled most.

'He's not feeling well and it can't be easy being cooped up in bed.'

Raff appreciated what Clara was trying to do but it was no good; her determined 'little miss sunshine' routine wasn't going to fix this.

'He practically accused you of being a gold-digger,' he pointed out. 'I shouldn't have let him speak to you like that.' He had been poised to walk out, stopped only by her calming hand on his arm, holding him in place, the pressure of her fingers warning him to keep still, keep quiet.

'I wasn't going anywhere.' Clara stopped as they reached the hospital foyer; the marbled floor, discreet wooden reception desk and comfortable seating areas gave it the air of an exclusive hotel—if you ignored the giveaway scent of disinfectant and steamed vegetables. 'I've been called worse.' A wounded expression flashed across her face, so fleeting Raff wasn't sure if he had imagined it.

'Thank you.' The words seemed inadequate. Despite his grandfather's antipathy she had been a dignified presence by his side, not too close, not clingy but affectionate and believable. He was torn between embarrassment that she had witnessed his grandfather's most petulant behaviour and an uncharacteristic gratitude for her silent support.

'No problem.' She was saying all the right things but her tone lacked conviction. 'It's my job after all.'

'Come on.' He needed to get out of here, away from the hospital, away from the toxic mixture of guilt and anger, to push it all firmly away. This was why he preferred to be abroad. He could be his own man out in the field. 'Let's go.'

Clara opened her mouth, about to ask where they were going, and then she slowly shut it again. At least they were in the centre of London—it might be a little damp but whatever Raff had in mind it was unlikely to involve mud.

And Raff obviously needed to blow off steam. He was keeping himself together but his jaw was clenched tight and a muscle was working in his cheek. Clara had been treated like dirt before, dismissed out of hand— but her own family had always been there to support her. She couldn't imagine her own grandfather looking at her with such cold, disappointed eyes. Even a teen pregnancy hadn't shaken his love and belief in her.

Polly had called Raff 'The Golden Boy' but it seemed

to her that his exalted position came with a heavy price. No wonder he had needed to employ Clara, to take some of the pressure his demanding grandfather was heaping on as he took advantage of his illness and frailty. An unexpected sympathy reverberated through her—Raff's need to be as far away from his family as possible was a little more understandable.

She kept pace with a silent, brooding Raff as he walked briskly through the busy streets expertly avoiding the crowds of tourists, the busy commuters and the loitering onlookers. Clara rarely visited London despite the direct rail link; if you asked her she would say she was too busy but the truth was it scared her. So noisy, so crowded, so unpredictable. The girl who once planned to travel the world was cowed by her own capital city.

But here, today, it felt different. Friendlier, more vibrant, the way it had felt when she was a teenager, down for the day to shop for clothes in Camden and hang out in Covent Garden where Maddie hoped to be talent-spotted by a model agency whilst Clara spent hours browsing in the specialist travel bookshop. Was it even still there? All her books and maps were boxed away at her parents' house. Maybe she should retrieve some of them, show them to Summer.

'I need to organise a nurse to look after him,' he said, breaking the lengthy silence. 'The hospital won't allow him home without one. He needs to have a specialist diet too, and he is going to hate that.' His mouth twisted. 'At this rate it's going to be weeks before I can talk about the company with him again.'

'Isn't there anyone else who can intercede? Your grandmother?'

Raff shook his head. 'They're separated. She'll have

a go, if I ask her to, but he's never quite forgiven her for leaving.'

Clara knew that Polly and Raff had been raised by their grandparents but not that they had split up. She swallowed, her throat tight; it was becoming painfully apparent how little she knew of Polly's life. They were supposed to be friends and yet she had no idea where she was or why she'd gone.

But was Clara any better? She didn't confide either, happy to keep the conversation light, to discuss work and plans but never feelings, never anything deep. Maybe that was why they were friends, both content with the superficial intimacy, their real fears locked safely away.

'Have they been split up long?'

'Nearly twelve years.' He gave her a wry smile. 'She waited until after Christmas our first year at university. Didn't want to spoil the holidays, she said. We were just amazed she made it that long. She'd wanted out for a long time.'

'I can't imagine your grandfather is easy to live with.' That was an understatement.

He huffed out a dry laugh. 'He's not. Poor Grandmother, from things she let slip I think she was on the verge of leaving when we came to live with them. She only stayed for Polly and me. Now she lives in central London and takes organised trips, volunteers at several museums and spends the rest of her time at the theatre or playing bridge. She's very happy.'

'What about your parents?' She flushed; curiosity had got the better of her. 'I'm sorry, I don't mean to pry.'

'That's okay. We are meant to be dating, after all, and none of this is exactly state secrets.' He didn't look okay though, his eyes shadowed, his mouth drawn into a straight line. 'My father had a stroke when we were eight.'

'I am so sorry.' Tentatively she reached out and touched his arm, awkward comfort. 'That must have been awful.'

'We thought he was sleeping. The ambulance man said if we had called 999 earlier...' His voice trailed off.

Cold chilled her, goosebumping her arms, her spine as his words hit her—they'd found their father collapsed? Her heart ached for the two small children who had to suddenly grow up in such a terrible way.

'The stroke was devastating.' There was a darkness in his voice, the sense of years of regret, of guilt. 'He had to go into a home—oh, the very best home, you know? All luxury carpets and plush chairs but we still knew, even at that age, that it was a place where people went to die.'

Clara felt for the familiar cold curve of her bangle and began to twist it automatically; she wanted to reach out and hold him, hold the small boy who had to watch his father disintegrate before his eyes.

'Our mother couldn't handle it,' Raff continued, still in that same bleak tone. 'She went away for a rest and just stayed away, So my grandparents stepped in, sent us to boarding school and gave us a home in the holidays—and my poor grandmother had to wait ten years for her escape.'

'Her choice.' Clara knew she sounded brisk, the way she sounded when encouraging Summer to sleep without a nightlight, to go on a school trip, to walk to the corner shop on her own. 'It was the right thing for her at the time. There's no point dwelling on what-might-have-beens. You go mad that way.'

She knew all about that. If she hadn't stayed in that particular hostel, hadn't met Byron. If she'd tried harder with his father, if she'd stayed in Australia. 'Our lives are littered with the paths not taken,' she said. 'But if we spend all our time staring wistfully at them we'll never see what's right in front of us.'

'A sick, unreasonable grandfather, a missing twin and an unwanted job?' But the dark note had gone from his voice and Clara was relieved to see a small smile playing around the firm mouth. He stopped in front of her and turned to look at the golden building in front of them. 'We're here. Welcome to the millstone round my neck.'

It had been a long time since Clara had set foot in Rafferty's. The flagship department store occupied a grand art deco building just off Bond Street and, although it was a little out of the way of the tourists pounding bustling Oxford Street and Regent Street, it was a destination in its own right. Discreet, classy and luxurious; just the name Rafferty's conjured up another era, an era of afternoon tea, cocktails and red, red lipstick.

Tourists flocked here, desperate to buy something, anything, so they could walk away with one of the distinctive turquoise and gold bags; socialites, It Girls and celebrities prowled the halls filled with designer items. Anyone who was anybody—and those who aspired to be—drank cocktails at the bar. Rafferty's was a well-loved institution, accessible glamour for anybody with money to spend.

As a child Clara had visited the store every Christmas to see the spectacular window displays, admire the lights, to confide her wish-list to Father Christmas. It had been one of the highlights of her year—and yet she had never brought Summer. She had never even made the seventy-five-minute-long journey into London with her daughter. London was too big, too noisy, too unpredictable.

But as she stood on the edge of the marble steps, re-membering the breathless excitement of those perfect days out, Clara's throat tightened. Choosing the perfect gift, admiring the other shoppers, having afternoon tea in the elegant restaurant, those memories meant Christmas to her. How could she not have passed those memories on to her daughter?

To keep Summer safe? Or to keep Clara herself safe?

Maybe, just maybe, she was a little overprotective.

'Are you going to stand there all day or are you actually coming in?'

Clara swallowed. It must be nice to be Raff Rafferty. Adored heir to all this. So sure of yourself, so confident that you could treat life as one big joke.

And yet there were contradictions there. She might disapprove of the lies he was feeding his grandfather—although after the cold, hostile meeting this morning she understood them. But what was he fighting for? The right to live on his trust fund? The right not to do a day's work?

Clara tried to remember what exactly Polly had told her about him. Not much, which was odd in itself; they were twins after all. She said he was spoilt, that she had to work three times as hard and still didn't receive equal recognition. That he was 'messing around abroad somewhere'. Clara had assumed that he was travelling, partying, having fun. After twenty-four hours in his company she wasn't so sure.

He was arrogant and annoying and treated life as one big joke but he didn't *seem* lazy, didn't seem careless of his family's ties and expectations. He had come running the second he'd thought Polly was in trouble and according to the nurse had spent three days and nights at his grandfather's bedside.

Yep, he was definitely a puzzle but, she reminded herself, he was none of her business. And none of this was real, no matter how surprisingly easy it was to forget that.

'I thought you went away to escape Rafferty's,' she said, walking up the famous curved steps to meet him.

'To escape *running* Rafferty's,' he corrected her, escorting her through the famous gilt and glass revolving doors with a light touch on her elbow.

As soon as he took his hand away the spot he had touched felt cold. Clara had to resist the temptation to rub it, to try and get the heat back.

They had entered a massive circular room topped with an ornate glass dome. It was the heart of Rafferty's, an iconic image, immortalised in film, photos and books. Looking up, Clara saw the famous galleries ringing the dome, three storeys of them. Each storey took up the entire block and was filled with a myriad of desirable items: food, clothes, jewellery, books, accessories, pictures, lamps, rugs.

Down here on the beautifully tiled ground floor the world's leading make-up and perfume brands plied their wares, stalls set out in a semi-circle around the foot of the dome. The middle was always reserved for themed displays and, at Christmas, the giant tree that dominated the room.

It was a wonderland. And the man standing next to her wanted to throw it all away.

'It's not that I'm not proud of Rafferty's,' he said, as if he could read her thoughts. 'It was like having our very own giant playground. We could go anywhere, do anything. Polly would walk around talking to all the staff, finding out what they did and how everything worked. I'd usually be hidden away with a stash of sugary contraband in a stock cupboard somewhere.'

'Sounds idyllic.' She could see it too, a cheeky-faced blond urchin charming his way through the store.

'It was,' he sighed, a faraway look in his eye. 'This was our real home. We held every birthday party here. I had my first kiss in this very room with Victoria Embleton-Jones. She was taller than me and a lot more sure of herself. I was in love for a whole week and then she dumped me for an older man with less sweaty hands and a car. I was devastated.'

'My heart's breaking. How old were you?'

'Fourteen. It took me a whole month to get over her. I still get nervous shakes when I meet anyone called Victoria.' His face was solemn but he couldn't hide the gleam dancing in his eyes.

Clara resisted the urge to snort. 'No wonder this place is so special to you, filled with such poignant memories.' She looked around at the bustling, chattering, spending throngs. 'I used to come here when I was a child.' It felt oddly like a confession. 'Afternoon tea was always a highlight of the holidays. I felt so sophisticated.' She sighed at the memory of delicate porcelain teapots and plates filled with cakes. Clara put a hand to her suddenly hollow stomach; it had been a long morning. 'Is that why we're here?' She tried not to sound too hopeful.

'It's not time for a tea break yet, Miss Castleton.' He shook his head. 'I don't know, can't get the staff these days. First we work and then we reward ourselves with as much cake as you can manage.'

'Work?' Heat washed over her; how had she misread the situation so badly? 'If you need a PA I can certainly supply one.'

'I have a perfectly good if rather terrifying PA. She disapproves of me almost as much as you do.' Raff grinned at her flushed and confused denial. 'No, it's time we went shopping.'

'Shopping? I do grocery shopping, as you know, presents as well, but I contract out personal shopping and interior designing…' She was babbling again but couldn't seem to stop.

'Look around, Clara. You're in the world's most famous department store. I could click my fingers and summon a personal shopper for almost anything you could imagine. No, we are going to get you some clothes.'

She gaped at him. 'I have clothes!'

Raff looked her over, sweeping her up and down assessingly. Clara had to fight every individual muscle to make it stay still; the urge to cover herself protectively, shield herself from those keen eyes, was almost overwhelming.

'You have suits,' he said finally. 'Sharp, businesslike suits. Which is great for the office but no use when you're with me. You have jeans and T-shirts and you have a few pretty dresses like the one you are wearing. That's all fine but none of that will do for black-tie dos, for cocktail parties or any of the other dull but apparently necessary events Polly wastes her free time at.'

'Cocktail parties?' The nearest Clara got to a cocktail party was trying to decide between red or white wine at Sunday lunch. 'I didn't expect…'

'I told you it would be time consuming.' His gaze was steely now. 'I also said I would pay you handsomely and make it worth your while in any way necessary. Unfortunately Rafferty's needs to be present at these events. Grandfather can't and Polly won't, until I track her down and beg her to come home. So it's down to me.'

He looked as if he would rather be sitting alone with Mr Simpkins.

'But you, Clara Castleton, are both my secret weapon and my shield. Your very presence will hopefully steer conversation away from dull topics like where I have been and what my plans are whilst simultaneously saving me from match-making mothers and their eager daughters. For that you need clothes. And luckily for you I am temporarily running an establishment that supplies pretty much any outfit you desire.'

'Wait a minute.' She eyed him suspiciously. 'Have you been sneaking through my things?' Raff's assessment of her wardrobe had been depressingly close to the mark.

Raff took another step closer and took her arm, the touch sending a jolt of electricity shooting up, settling at the base of her stomach, his proximity making every nerve buzz. 'I don't need to. I started working here when I was fourteen and spent at least six months in every department.' He shot her an amused grin. 'I was very successful in ladies' wear.'

'That doesn't surprise me,' she muttered.

'So if you're ready...' he ignored the interruption '...let's shop.'

'You will make someone a very good husband one day.' Clara eyed the rail of clothes that Raff and Susannah, the personal shopper he had co-opted to help them, had picked out. 'Forget the name and fortune, any man who can shop like you will be snapped up.'

Raff leant back against the wall. In a stark contrast to the opulence of the outer store the private changing rooms, exclusively for the use of those rich or lucky enough to secure the services of a personal shopper, were a study in sleek minimalism. The walls were a steely grey, the sofas chic, uncomfortable-looking studies in white and black; in this environment the clothes were the stars.

'It's a good thing one of us showed some interest,' he said. 'Poor Susannah certainly earned her commission today. I don't think she's ever met anyone who dislikes clothes as much as you do.'

Clara bit just as he knew she would. 'I like clothes well enough,' she said indignantly. 'I'm just not into fancy clothes or fancy designers or fancy prices.'

Raff suppressed a smile. He might be playing fairy godfather but this Cinderella wasn't at all interested. She'd probably be far more comfortable cleaning the hearth and making the pumpkin into pies than going to the ball.

'Or fancy shoes...' he said provocatively.

'If feet were supposed to be that elevated...' Clara began.

'Then our bone structure would be quite different,' he finished. 'I know, you told me at least three times and poor Susannah twenty. Normally women weep with gratitude after she supplies them with shoes, not lecture her about osteology. Come on, Cinders, enjoy the glass slippers.'

'Cinderella probably almost broke her neck rushing down those stairs in just one shoe.'

She wasn't giving an inch. He shook his head, his grin wide. 'Fairy tales must be a barrel of laughs at your house. It's important that you play the part well and that means dressing the part too. You don't have to keep any of it after we're finished: sell them and give the proceeds to charity, turn them into bunting. They're yours. Personally I'd say enjoy them. There must be a huge demand for sequinned shifts in Hopeford.'

Her mouth tilted upwards. Her smile was irresistible;

maybe it was a good thing she didn't unleash it often. 'Oh, there is. Perfect for a quiet drink at The Swan.'

'We don't have to take them all,' he pointed out. 'I think you need about six cocktail dresses, the same amount in day dresses and shoes and bags as well. Come on, Cinders, the sooner you try them on and make some decisions, the sooner you can have that cake.'

'I think I preferred the mud,' Clara said, but she unhooked the silver sequinned shift and began to carry it to the curtained-off area at the back. She paused at the curtain and turned back, her eyes lowered, cheeks flushed. 'I feel really uncomfortable about this, Raff, you buying me these clothes. It's one thing paying me for my time but this feels a step too far.' She raised her eyes, meeting his with obvious difficulty. 'I can't begin to offer to pay you for them. I'm sure that I can manage with what I have.'

Raff found himself short of breath, unable to formulate any kind of reply. He had been out with enough women to consider that he had a pretty good grip on the feminine mind even if he had been thrust into a single-sex school long before puberty, but he hadn't seen this coming.

Not one ex, from the trust fund socialite to the vegan gardener, had ever turned down a free outfit from Rafferty's.

He wasn't sure whether he admired her pride—or found her stubbornness frustrating. 'Well technically I won't be buying you anything, they're a gift from Rafferty's, but remember I'm not playing Professor Higgins,' he said as offhandedly as he could. 'I'm just ensuring you have the right outfits for the job I have hired you to do. I supply the, what did you call them? Instruments of torture? You wear them.'

She looked at him searchingly for a long moment before nodding, a short reluctant agreement. 'Of course,' she grumbled, 'these clothes aren't designed for real women. If I was a size-zero giraffe I might find this easier.'

Raff ran his eyes over her approvingly. Clara wasn't built like a model, it was true, nor did she eat like one, thank goodness. The year after university, full of pent-up energy he couldn't expel at work, he had partied hard and dated several models and socialites. He had soon got bored with the shallow crowd he was running with.

And women who thought a piece of lettuce meant a full dinner.

No, give him someone like Clara, not too tall, not too small, curves in all the right places. That shift she was holding, for instance, it would fall to mid-thigh, showcase those fantastic legs, cling to the curve of her bosom.

The room felt very small, just a curtain separating him from the area where Clara would be unbuttoning all those tiny buttons, slipping her dress off, replacing it with the short shift.

He took in a deep breath. It was warm in here, roasting in fact. He should talk to someone about the temperature.

'I think you'll look perfect,' he said hoarsely. 'Why don't you get started? I'll just be...' He waved at the entrance. 'I need to get something.' A brandy, a cold shower, some air.

Left alone, Clara felt curiously deflated. There had been something in Raff's eyes. Something hot, something terrifyingly honest. Something that had awakened feelings she had spent so long hiding from: what it was like to be wanted, what it was like to want.

Clara sank down into the hard-backed chair, the sole

piece of furniture in the spacious curtained-off area. For the first time in a really long time she wished she had someone to lean on, to confide in.

Raff, Byron's impending visit, deciding how to best use the money Raff was paying her. There was so much going on she didn't know where to turn.

But there was no one. She didn't want to worry her mother, Summer was too young, Maddie so busy. She had nobody. It hit her like a blow to the stomach as hot, unwanted tears pricked at the backs of her eyes; she blinked them away, wrapping her arms around herself as if she could ward off the unwanted knowledge. She would be so ashamed if her mother or cousin or the handful of friends she kept in contact with guessed just how she felt.

Lonely.

'Come on, Clara, where will self-pity get you?' She hadn't succumbed when she found out she was pregnant, only eighteen, thousands of miles away from home. She had stayed strong when Byron walked out of her life a month before their baby was born.

She wouldn't, *couldn't* give in now. She had a wonderful, healthy daughter, a thriving business. She was lucky, even if it was hard to remember that sometimes.

Slowly, feeling a little punch drunk, Clara rose to her feet and began to unbutton her dress. She was here to do a job. Feelings had nothing to do with it.

The shift was heavy and yet it felt wonderfully cool and soft against her skin, the sequins sparkling as the spotlights hit it. Reflected in the many mirrors that lined the room, Clara gave in to the temptation to pirouette, loving the way the fabric flattered her. Raff was right: annoyingly, she did feel more confident, more sociable in this fabulous, exorbitantly expensive dress.

Muttering, she forced her feet into a pair of strappy

heels. She had thought that pairing silver shoes with a silver dress would be too much, that she would end up resembling a giant glitterball, but she had been wrong. The outfit looked amazing even with bare, pale legs, minimal make-up and a ponytail. Her stomach fluttered at the thought of really going out dressed like this; hair, make-up, accessories. Raff on her arm.

If she could just walk in the shoes that would be a considerable bonus.

A rustle from the other side of the curtain alerted her to another person's presence. Raff must have returned.

Clara took another look in the mirror. Was that really her? So elegant? The shoes added another four inches to her height, giving her legs the illusion of endless length. The urge to hide, tear off this costume and become her own safe self again was almost overwhelming but Clara sucked in a deep breath. She *would* walk through the curtain; she *would* show Raff.

She would hopefully see that heat in his eyes again.

Heart hammering, the wobble in her step not solely caused by the unfamiliar heels, Clara pulled the curtain open, a self-deprecating remark on her lips. But there was no need to utter it.

The room was empty. Another rail of clothes and matching accessories had joined the first one.

Her stomach plummeted as the adrenaline disappeared. It must have been Susannah she had heard. 'Fool,' she muttered. Clara chewed her cheek, indecisive. Should she wait, try on something else, look for him? Unsure, she walked to the door and peeked out, worry turning to irritation as she saw him, right in front of the door, deep in conversation with a small brunette who was smiling up at him.

'Clara?' Darn it, he had spotted her. 'Sorry, I bumped

into an old colleague.' Was it her imagination or did he hesitate over the word 'colleague'?

'Hi, I'm Lisa.' The brunette smiled over at Clara. 'It's so great to see Raff. I thought he was in Afghanistan.'

She thought what? Beach bum or adrenaline junkie, either way Afghanistan was the last place Clara imagined Raff Rafferty.

Or was it? A picture flashed into her mind. That first afternoon, his face grey with weariness, the kind of weariness from hours and hours of travel, sitting in trucks and small airport waiting rooms not from the pampered world of First Class. The battered jeans, the old kitbag.

None of it had added up at the time but she'd been so convinced that she knew the man she was dealing with she hadn't even stopped to consider that her preconceptions might be skewed.

'No, not this time,' he said with a quick glance over at Clara. Was that embarrassment in his eyes? 'I was in Jordan. We're trying to make sure there are some medical facilities in the camps there but I was needed at home so had to take some leave. How about you?'

Lisa blushed. 'I'm based back in the UK at the moment. Did you know I married Mike, Dr Hardy?'

'I had heard. Congratulations. I did a brief stint with him out in Somalia. He's a great bloke.' Again a swift, almost pleading glance at Clara.

Somalia, Afghanistan, Jordan? Polly had said that Raff was abroad, she had been dismissive, giving Clara the impression that he was partying on a beach somewhere, not working in some of the most dangerous places in the world. Wasn't she worried about him?

'Mike is setting up a paediatric programme here in London for kids that just can't be treated in the field so I'm based here too now. It's not the same but there's a lot to do. Actually…' Lisa eyed him speculatively '…this could be a massive piece of luck running into you like this. What are you doing in five weeks' time? Will you still be here?'

'I think so. Why?'

Lisa clasped her hands together and looked up at Raff hopefully. 'We're holding a fundraising ball, all the great and the good digging deep, you know the kind of thing! We had Phil lined up to speak but he had to pull out. Could you speak in his place?'

Raff shifted from foot to foot, his expression one of deep discomfort. Clara watched him with some amusement.

Good, she thought, *let him get out of this.*

'People don't want to hear from me,' he said eventually. 'They want to hear from the medical teams. They're the ones with the real stories.'

'We have doctors and nurses and helicopter pilots and patients,' Lisa assured him. 'But no one understands that without you guys there wouldn't be a hospital— or water or electricity or a single bed. Turning a dusty piece of desert into a hospital? That's the real heroism. We just turn up when it's ready for us. Don't you agree?' she asked Clara.

Clara looked at Raff with her most innocent expression. 'I really do,' she said. 'He'll be there, don't worry. I guarantee it.'

'Really? That's brilliant. Raff, come along to the office this week and we'll sort out slides and I'll let you know how long you have to speak for. Make it funny but real as well, try and make them cry. That's always worth a few more noughts on the cheque!'

'I'll see what I can do.' He slid his gaze over to Clara. 'I'm sure Clara will be happy to help me. You'll have a bit longer to wait for that cake though, Clara. You need a dress fit for a ball, and a pair of glass slippers too.' His eyes dropped to her feet, wobbling in the thin-heeled sandals. 'I'll tell Susannah to bring the highest she can find.'

CHAPTER SIX

CLARA UNZIPPED THE silver shift and let it spill to the floor. She knew Raff was on the other side of the curtain but his silence was absolute.

Fine, if that was the way he wanted to play it, there was no way she was going to be the one to crack.

She bent down and picked up the dress, carefully putting it on the hanger. Still no sound, not even a sigh. Anticipation clenched at her stomach as she slipped the next outfit, a wide-skirted silk affair in a vivid green, off the rail and put it on, barely bothering to check the mirror before wrenching the curtain aside.

'And?'

He was sitting on the sofa, lounging back seemingly without a care in the world. 'The shoes don't go.'

'They go with the other dress. I didn't change them.' Seriously? Shoes? That was what he was thinking? She wouldn't ask, she wouldn't, she wouldn't… 'Okay. Spill.' For goodness' sake, her self-control was legendary. She prided herself on it! But the need to know was burning her and she didn't want to examine why. 'Who was that?'

Raff got to his feet with leonine grace and sauntered over to the rail. 'I think we agreed on the red shoes for that outfit, didn't we? It'll work very well for lunches.

What?' He was regarding her with faint surprise. No wonder. Clara was aware she resembled a fishwife more than a lady-who-lunches, hands on hips and head back. 'I did introduce you. That was Lisa. We worked together.'

'Yes, in Somalia,' Clara said as patiently as she could manage. 'Why were you in Somalia?'

'I worked with her husband in Somalia,' Raff corrected her. 'I knew Lisa in Sri Lanka. I think...' he finished doubtfully. 'It might have been Bangladesh.'

'Mercenary or spy?' The words burst out before she could stop them.

'What?' The look of utter shock on his face was almost comical.

'You keep quiet about what you do, you work in some of the most dangerous places on earth, it has to be one or the other.' It was the only thing that made sense.

'Because spies and mercenaries love to throw fundraising balls?' How she hated that amused smile. He had of course honed in on the only flaw in her thinking.

'Part of your cover.' Okay, not the best idea she'd ever had.

'Interesting theory. I like it. I always fancied myself as a suave, martini-drinking type. Sorry to burst your little fantasy but nothing so exciting.' He paused and handed her another dress, a fifties-style halterneck that Clara secretly rather liked. 'Here, try this on. I'm a project manager for Doctors Everywhere.'

Oh.

Kitbags, dangerous places, fundraising balls, hospitals. That made sense. Reluctantly Clara let go of her visions of chase scenes, fancy cars, an evil mastermind bent on world domination.

'Doctors Everywhere?' she echoed as she obediently accepted the outfit and tottered her way back to the curtain.

Of course she had heard of them; they provided healthcare in the Third World, in refugee camps, in war spots.

They were incredibly well respected. Not the natural playground of playboys. Which meant that every little preconception she had was wrong.

Clara changed on autopilot, so many thoughts tumbling around her brain it was as if her head had joined the circus.

Somehow the emotion she could most easily identify was anger. She pushed away the thought that this might be a little unreasonable. After all, what Raff Rafferty did with his time was really none of her business.

He had made it her business, she argued back as she fumbled with the buttons at the back and cautiously zipped up the tight bodice. Employing her, introducing her to his grandfather, buying her these exquisite, over-priced, really very flattering clothes.

He had made her complicit.

The curtain made a most satisfying swoosh as she pulled it open, and she stomped forward only wobbling twice. Damn, she was still wearing the stupid sliver shoes. No wonder Cinderella had discarded her glass slippers; she was probably in agony by midnight.

'Doctors Everywhere?'

'Yep.' He was still standing up, leaning against the back wall. The plain colour of the backdrop suited him, made the hair a little blonder, the eyes even bluer. Not that she was noticing. Not at all.

Oh, no, she was putting her hands on her hips again. Ten years of careful, calm control and yet one day with this man and she was unleashing her inner harpy. 'Which is obviously such a terrible thing for you to do you had no choice but to lie to your sister and grandfather?' Clara could hear the sarcasm dripping from her voice and tried to calm down.

This wasn't her family. Why did she care so much?

He looked at her for one long moment and Clara thought he wasn't going to answer. After all, the annoying voice of reason whispered, he didn't have to explain himself to her, but after a moment he sighed. 'I didn't lie. They know what I do.'

'They *know*? Then why does your grandfather want you to take over Rafferty's? And why has Polly never mentioned it?' Clara twisted the heavy curtain fabric around her hand and studied him curiously.

'According to Grandfather it's just a phase I'll grow out of. As for Polly...' He glanced away, staring at the stark walls as if the answer would be found there. 'I don't know what she hates more—that Grandfather always wanted me to have this place or that I *don't* want it. I hoped that if I went away she would be able to convince him that she was the better candidate but she accused me of running away. Maybe she was right.'

'Why?' So she was curious; it wasn't a crime.

He pushed himself off the wall and walked over to the small table, which held a jug of iced water and a bunch of grapes, nothing that could mark the valuable clothes. 'Want one?' he offered and she shook her head.

He poured himself a glass. Clara watched as he took a long, deep drink, her eyes drawn to the way his tanned throat worked as he swallowed. He set the glass down and, with a purposeful manner, as if he had come to some kind of internal decision, he turned and faced her squarely, eyes holding hers.

'Because I *was* running away,' he said. 'Away from expectations and responsibility and guilt and family. I was at a really low point, Polly and I were fighting,

Grandfather kept promoting me higher and higher whilst passing her over—and believe me it wasn't on merit—and then I met up with a friend who was volunteering with Doctors Everywhere. He mentioned that they always needed people with good project-management skills and a second language—to be honest I didn't think I had a chance. A pampered boy like me who thought travelling second class was slumming it?

'Nobody was as surprised as me when they took me. But I didn't ever consider not going.' He grimaced. 'I genuinely thought it was a one-off. That I'd be back in three months relieved to be back behind my desk.' His mouth twisted with a wry humour as he remembered. 'I nearly was. That first three months was the most difficult, stressful three months of my life. It made prep school seem like a holiday camp. I couldn't wait for it to be over.

'But I signed up for my next assignment the day after I was released.' He shrugged. 'I didn't know then that I had been broken in easy—an existing brick-built hospital, my own bedroom, not a war zone. Somalia was a horrid shock. But I signed up again as soon as I returned from there, for six months that time. It's like a drug. I think I can walk away any time but I always go back for more.

'Because…it makes a real difference, Clara. Everything I did changed somebody's world. I might not be the person performing the operations—but I was the person making sure that the operations could take place. That we had beds and kits and food and water. It mattered.'

'And Rafferty's doesn't?'

'Not to me.'

Raff heard his words echo around the room. He'd thought them many times but had never said them aloud.

But the sky didn't fall in, the world didn't end, his

grandfather didn't appear in a puff of smoke to blast him away like a vengeful god. He was still the same man, still standing there.

Only everything had changed. He couldn't fool himself or his family any longer. He wasn't working away for a sabbatical or a career break or for an adventure. It was what he *did*, what he needed to do, what he was. And it didn't matter whether his grandfather left him Rafferty's or not, he would just sign it over to Polly. It was hers; she deserved it.

There was no point waiting and hoping that things would work out his way; he had to make them happen.

Clara was still looking at him, that green gaze of hers intent. He didn't know what he had expected. Shock? Disapproval? Horror? It was hard to remember sometimes that to other people Rafferty's was no more than a place to buy beautifully gift-wrapped socks or get an expensive but perfect afternoon tea. It wasn't the centre of everyone's world.

What was it about this woman that made him want to confess, to spill all the secrets that he preferred to keep locked away so tightly? Was it her directness, her transparency? The unexpected way she lit up when she smiled?

Their eyes were locked, the colour rising faint on her cheeks, her breath coming a little quicker. The full mouth parted slightly. Heat rose through him, sudden and shocking. The walls of the room seemed to contract; all he could see was her. The red-gold hair tumbling around her creamy shoulders, delicate tempting shoulders exposed by the deceptively demure halterneck dress, shoulders that were begging for a man to touch them, to kiss the triangle of freckles delicately placed like an old-fashioned patch.

Raff swallowed, blood thrumming round his body, his heartbeat accelerating. She was so very close, green eyes darkening until they resembled the storm-tossed sea. Just a few short steps…

'That suits you.' Raff jumped as Susannah heeled in a third rail. 'Although I don't think those are the right shoes.'

Clara pulled her eyes from his, pulling at the hem of the dress. The room felt a good ten degrees colder and suddenly a lot bigger. 'No,' she agreed, throwing Raff a faint, complicit smile that warmed him through. 'After ten minutes in these shoes I am completely convinced that they are absolutely not the right shoes.'

'Have you made any decisions yet? I've brought a few formal evening gowns as Mr Raff instructed.' Susannah gestured towards the rail. 'He didn't specify but with your colouring I thought greens, blacks and golds might be most suitable. Do you want me to stay and help you try them on?' She picked up a long, dark dress and carried it into the curtained area, hanging it onto one of the silver rails that hung between the floor-length mirrors.

'That's very kind but I think I'll manage, thanks. They all look lovely.' Clara threw the rail a helpless look. 'I'm only on my third dress. I'd better hurry up or I'll never get my reward.'

Cake, she meant cake, Raff reminded himself, fingers curling into a fist as other, equally sweet ways of rewarding her flashed through his head.

Clara took a step back, retreating behind the curtain as Susannah left. Raff paced around the room trying not to interpret every sound he heard. The rustle of a button, the slow, steady zip as the dress was undone, the faint slither of material falling to the floor.

Maybe he should have some more water.

'Have you ever tried to tell them how you feel?' Her voice floated through the curtain.

It took a few seconds for the words to penetrate through his brain, for him to remember the conversation they had been halfway through before time slowed, before his brain had gone into lockdown and his body into overdrive.

'No,' he admitted, running one hand through his hair. It was a relief in some ways to spill the feelings he had carried around for so long, locked inside so tight he barely recognised them himself. Clara was unconnected; she was safe.

In this context at least.

And she was invisible, hidden away behind the curtain; it felt as if he had the seal of the confessional. That he could say anything and be absolved.

'Rafferty's means everything to Grandfather, to Polly too. But it bores me. Merchandise and pricing and advertising and thinking about Christmas in June,' he said slowly, trying to pick his words carefully as he articulated the feelings he barely admitted to himself. 'Polly and I owe my grandfather everything and all he wanted, all he wants, is for me to take this place over. To take my father's place by continuing his work, accepting my great-grandfather's legacy. I didn't know how to tell him I didn't want it. Not ever. What kind of spoiled brat breaks his grandfather's heart?'

She didn't reply. How could she? But her silence didn't feel hostile or loaded.

'I tried.' He leant back against the wall and gazed unseeingly at the ceiling, the long years of thwarted hopes and unwanted expectations heavy on his conscience. 'I really, really tried, worked here after school and every holiday, gave up my dreams of studying medicine and struggled through three years of business management instead. I even did an MBA and I took up the role awaiting me here—and every day, for six years, I hated coming to work.'

He sighed. 'But ironically Polly loved it. I hoped that if Grandfather saw how well she did then he would switch his attention to her. But he's old-fashioned. He doesn't even realise how much he's hurt her by leaving the company to me.'

'You have to tell him.' She sounded so matter of fact. As if it were that easy.

'I know. Unfortunately last time I tried he ended up in hospital.' Raff tried to make his voice sound light but he knew he was failing.

'What's your plan? To spend another six years here hating every moment, you miserable, Polly miserable?'

'No!' he protested. Her words cut a little deeper than he liked. After all, he *had* taken the path of least resistance, hoping it would all work out somehow. He had only postponed the inevitable.

He had run through every possible conversation in his head. None of them ever ended well. If he had to he would just walk away, refuse to be involved, but the old man had lost one son already. If only there was a way to keep the family together and live his own life.

If only he could make his grandfather see…

Unless…

'I could invite him to the ball,' he said, his brain beginning to tick over with ideas. 'Let him see for himself what I've been up to.'

'Will he be fit?' She didn't sound convinced.

There was the flaw. 'It's five weeks away. He'll be back home this week and resting. If I make sure he's escorted at all times, order a special low-fat dinner and keep him away from the wine he should be okay. He never was the sort to dance the night away. I could take a table, fill it with business cronies. He'd enjoy that.'

'And then what?' She still sounded doubtful.

He was over thirty. It was time to be a man, banish the guilt-ridden small boy, eager to please whatever the cost. 'Then, after the ball, when he's seen the difference we make, the difference I make, I'll talk to him again. Honestly and firmly.'

It wasn't a foolproof plan by any means. Nor was it an instant answer. Raff would have to stick around for nearly two months—but he'd planned for that after all, booked Clara for up to six weeks.

It felt like the best shot he had. And regardless of whatever his grandfather decided his own decision was made.

It was only now that he realised just how heavy his burden had been: guilt, expectations, responsibility weighing him down. He wasn't free of it, not yet, but freedom was in sight. It was strange how talking it through with someone, sharing his burden, had helped.

Would anyone have done or was it Clara herself? Raff wasn't sure he wanted to explore that thought any further.

'It could work.' She sounded a little more enthusiastic. 'You better make sure your presentation is spectacular.'

'Our presentation,' he said silkily. 'You're the one who promised we'd be there, agreed to all this. I want your help with every aspect. You don't just get to turn up late and leave early, Cinders. You have to work for your dress and glass slippers.'

Talking of which, she had been a long time getting changed. 'Are you okay in there?'

'Ah...' she sounded embarrassed '...is Susannah there?'

'No, why?'

'Can you find her?' Embarrassment was replaced with curt impatience.

Raff's mouth quirked. 'Are you in need of help? Maybe I can assist? I am fully trained, remember?'

'Raff Rafferty, please find Susannah right now.'

Grinning, Raff sauntered to the door and looked around. No sign. 'I can't see her,' he called. 'I can page her but she might be at the other end of the building, or I can help. Your choice.'

He could almost hear the wheels turning as Clara deliberated her choices.

'Okay. But not one quip, and no looking.'

Interesting.

'I'm a professional,' he assured her. But he didn't feel professional as he walked over; he felt more like an over-eager schoolboy who'd been promised an over-the-bra fumble. Inappropriate, he scolded himself.

And yet he couldn't stop thinking about creamy, bare shoulders and those three little freckles.

Deep breath. Focus on the job at hand. Raff pulled the curtain a little to one side and stepped into the changing room.

Where he stopped still. He didn't want to stare, he knew it was wrong and yet, and yet…

'Well, don't just stand there.' Clara gestured to her side. 'Help me. It's stuck and have you seen the price tag? I can't exactly yank it.'

She was wearing a floor-length strapless dress in a shade of blue so dark it almost looked black.

Revealing both her shoulders and a generous amount of cleavage, the dress clung as tightly as a second skin, emphasising the dip at her waist, the curve of her bottom, the length of her legs. Raff swallowed.

'The zip,' she said with killing emphasis as he remained static. 'It's stuck.'

Trying, with little success, to get some air into his suddenly oxygen-deprived lungs, Raff walked over. It seemed to take an eternity. He was a fool, to think he could walk in here, to the intimacy of a room where clothes were discarded, a room of lingerie and limbs and clinging silks. A fool to think he could step so close to naked arms, inhale the light floral scent she wore, watch one curl tumble down onto a bare shoulder. To touch her.

'Just here.' Hadn't she noticed the effect she was having on him? 'Can you see?'

Raff put one hand onto her ribs, holding her still as with utter concentration his other hand worked at the tiny zip, trying to free it from the thread that held it prisoner. Her skin was hot, burning him through the silk; he wasn't sure whether he could really hear her heart hammering or whether it was his imagination.

Or if it was his heart he heard, deafening him with its beat.

'I think I've got it.' His voice was gruff. 'There!'

As he freed the thread the zip shot down with alarming ease, his hand skimming her waist, her hip, and as it did so the top of the dress collapsed into graceful folds.

It all happened so fast, Clara didn't manage to grab at the dress or shield herself, and he, God help him, he didn't look away.

I'm sorry, he wanted to say, wanting to turn, to walk away, allow her a chance to get herself together but he was glued to the spot, desire hot, sweet and dark burning through him. She was perfect, the swell of her breasts, the dip of her waist, the faint silvery marks on her lower belly a badge of motherhood.

She should pull the dress up, turn away, slap his face,

scream, at least, at the very least she should cover herself up. She didn't even sunbathe topless and here she was, standing like a glamour model, exposed.

Only she was paralysed by the heat in his eyes, warming her through from head to toe, settling in the pit of her stomach, awakening a sweet, insistent ache she hadn't felt for so long. The naked desire in his face provoking pride, need, want.

And she wanted him too. She'd wanted him since the moment he had sauntered into her office, arrogant and demanding, making her think and making her do and making her feel. Not just because he looked so good, was so tall and so broad and so solid, not just because he had eyes that caressed and a mouth that made her knees tremble, but because he was a man who cared, hide it as he might.

But he was a man who was leaving. A man with itchy feet, who lived his life on the edge of civilisation, risking his life every day.

Right now it was hard to remember why that was a problem.

For all the strength apparent in him, held tightly coiled in that strong, muscled body, Clara knew she had all the control here. One look, one word and he would walk away with a sincere apology.

But one move forward and… Anticipation shivered through her.

She had spent the last ten years playing it safe, hiding from any experience that might test her, pouring all her emotions into motherhood. But the moment she had swung off that platform yesterday, the moment she had agreed to Raff Rafferty's offer, a new world had opened up. Not safe, not cosy, unplanned, a world that made her pulse beat and her blood hum and desire swirl sweetly inside her like honey.

And, oh, how she wanted.

Without thinking, without planning, she took another step forward, allowing the dress to fall to the ground as she did so. A wanton part of Clara, long locked away, smiled; the rest of her shivered in anticipation as she took in the expression on his face as Raff drank every inch of her in: fierce, hot need.

She felt utterly desirable.

Another step and she was close, so close. Millimetres separated them. Clara was trembling, tiny, anticipatory shivers running through her every nerve and sinew, her veins humming with excitement. She looked up at him boldly, allowing her want to shine out, and with a muffled growl Raff moved forward, closing the infinitesimal gap, pulling her hard against him. Clara found herself on her tiptoes, straining towards him.

It could only have been a second, two at the most before his lips touched hers but it felt like an eternity and Clara was sure she would explode if he didn't kiss her right there and then. And then his mouth was on hers sure and sweet, his hands were holding her close, one on the small of her back, holding her tight, the other in the nape of her neck and Clara wanted to climb onto him, into him and never let go. The lazy circles his fingers were making on her back, each one teasing hot, sensitised skin to the point of insanity, the way his hand cupped her tender neck, fingers buried in her hair, the way his mouth claimed her, demanding, expecting, giving.

Nothing had ever felt so right.

And when he let her go, staggered back with a look of total disbelief on his face, she was utterly bereft. 'The door's unlocked.' He was breathing hard, his voice ragged.

It took a moment for his words to penetrate her overheated brain. 'Oh.' Anyone could have come in, seen her practically naked, draped all over him. She should feel shamed. But she wasn't; she just wanted to be back in his arms, fused into him.

'I could lock it…'

Her eyes fastened on him, on the question implicit in eyes darkened by desire.

'You could, you probably should.' It wasn't the most eloquent response but it was all he needed. Powerful long strides across the room and the key was turned firmly, the outside world shut away.

Raff turned, eyes glittering dangerously. 'Clara?'

This was it, this was her chance to turn back, to get this relationship back on a professional footing. There was nothing she wanted less. 'I'm standing here in my underwear,' she said as calmly as she could, allowing a purr to enter her voice, tossing her hair back over her shoulder. 'And you're all the way over there and fully dressed…'

'That,' he said grimly, advancing on her with meaningful intent, 'can soon be remedied.'

Clara found herself being walked backwards until her back hit the wall. Panting, she looked up at him, a teasing smile on her lips, a smile he claimed as he swung Clara up in strong arms and she gave in to the sensation of his mouth, his hands, all thoughts drifting away and instinct taking over until she was no longer sure who she was or where she was. All she knew was that right now, in this moment, she was his.

CHAPTER SEVEN

'ARE YOU ENJOYING YOURSELF?'

'Yes, thank you.' Polite, cool, collected. Of course she was, just as she always was.

Clara was playing her part to perfection. His house, his life were seamlessly run by her employees while she stepped into her role as his girlfriend with grace. His employees liked her, she had charmed every business associate he had introduced her to and even his grandfather was showing signs of thawing.

But as soon as they were alone she retreated behind a shield of courtesy and efficiency. A shield he made no attempt to push aside.

It was better that way even if he did keep getting flashbacks of hot kisses, silky skin and fevered moans. After all, he usually kept his relationships short and sweet, superficial. Just not usually this short.

Or this sweet.

'I think we've shown our faces long enough if you want to leave.' Raff liked music as much as the next man but the benefit for ill and destitute musicians was a little out of his comfort zone. 'Unless, of course, you're enjoying it.'

The corners of her mouth tilted up, as close as she had got to a genuine smile in weeks. 'The violinist sounds just like Summer when she's practising,' she whispered, her breath sweet on his cheek. 'I had no idea I was raising a musical genius.'

'He sounds like Mr Simpkins when I've forgotten his evening fish,' Raff retorted. 'I think they're trying to extort money from us with menaces. Pay up or the music continues.'

'The percussionists were good and the harpist wasn't too bad…' She broke off, biting her lip, laughter lurking in her eyes.

'Until she started singing.' Raff glared over at the harp. 'If she isn't some sort of banshee then that voice was genetically engineered for warfare. There's no way those howls could be natural.'

'Come on.' Clara placed her hand upon his arm, just as she had done at every party, every dinner, every benefit over the last few weeks. His blood began to heat up until he was surprised his sleeve didn't burst into flames, but he didn't betray his discomfort by a single twinge.

'Only if you want,' he demurred. 'There's still the Cymbal Concerto to go. I'd hate for you to miss out.'

'So considerate.' She might look as if she were wafting along on his arm but her hand was inexorably steering him towards the open doors. 'Successful night?'

'When it was quiet enough to hear myself speak. Polly must be exhausted, spending her free time at these things.' Raff routinely worked twelve-, fourteen-hour days out in the field but give him those any day over his sister's routine of office by day, business socialising by night. 'I would give anything for a quiet night in The Swan.'

'Me too. You know, I thought my life was in danger of getting into a rut.' Clara breathed in a deep sigh as they left through the double doors that led from the ornate banqueting hall into the equally ornate but much quieter and cooler vestibule. 'But after several weeks of social events I am yearning for my sofa, a film and something really plain to eat. A jacket potato, salad, a piece of grilled chicken.'

'That sounds amazing.' It really did. Canapés and fancy dinners had lost any novelty after just a few days. 'Can I join you?'

It was supposed to be a joke but he made the mistake of looking directly at her; their gazes snagged, held and colour rose over the high cheekbones. 'It would be a rom-com,' she warned him, looking away, her voice light.

'My favourite.' Right then he almost meant it; a night lazing on a sofa, something undemanding on the TV, sounded like paradise. But he could feel the phone in his pocket almost physically weighting him down stuffed as it was with commitments and appointments and functions, all as serious and important and necessary as tonight's. 'I might have a spare evening in, oh, about three weeks.'

Rafferty's had to be represented, had to be seen to be there. This was where business was discussed, decided, where deals were struck. Under the sparkling lights, a glass of something expensive in one hand, a canapé in the other.

'Actually...' Clara sounded almost shy, tentative, completely unlike her usual assertive self '...I wondered if you were free tomorrow morning?'

'On a Sunday?' Raff didn't even try to hide his shock. Apart from that very first week, Clara had kept Sundays sacrosanct. They were her family day, a day she was very firmly off duty.

Did that mean her daughter would be there? Raff rubbed the back of his neck, suddenly a little warm. Just because he and Clara had shared a moment didn't mean he was ready to play at happy families. Especially as that particular moment had been well and truly brushed under the carpet.

And although there were times when he wished it hadn't been quite so rigorously filed under 'let's never mention this again', this was a stark reminder why it had to be.

Families, children, commitment. All very nice in principle, but tying. Even more weighty than the phone.

'I know we don't usually work on a Sunday.' She made the statement sound like a question and Raff shrugged non-committally.

It was chilly outside, cold enough for Clara to pull her wrap around her shoulders as they exited the building and began to make their way down the wide stone steps into the brightness of a London night. If the stars were out Raff couldn't see them, the streetlamps and neon signs colluding to hide the night sky from the city dwellers.

He had arranged to meet their driver on the corner of the street and steered Clara along the cobbled pavement, waiting for the inevitable comment about how much her feet hurt.

It didn't come. 'I have an appointment,' she said instead, looking down at the uneven cobbles. 'I wondered if you would come with me. You said, a few weeks ago...' Her voice trailed off.

'Yes.' He frowned as he remembered. 'Of course.' He *had* said he would attend a meeting with her. Only, that was before.

People *must* be talking about them, about the amount of time they were spending together, about the way he picked her up almost nightly in a chauffeur-driven car—maybe it was his turn to act the graceful escort. Only, it seemed worse somehow. Her family were so close, it felt deceitful.

The thought of getting to know her family, of possibly being accepted by them, twisted his stomach. What if he liked them? Or God forbid felt at home?

'It was the only day they offered me.' She finally looked up, her face pale, her features standing out starkly from the almost unnatural pallor of her skin.

'They?'

She took a deep breath, her body almost shaking. 'Summer's father isn't involved. It's his choice. I really tried.' Raff had to take a deep breath of his own to dampen down a sudden, shocking anger. How could anyone have left her to raise a child on her own?

'I send him photos, videos, school reports, tried to get him to Skype with her. He's never been that interested. But a few weeks ago, the day you asked me to help you out, he emailed.'

'He wants to see you tomorrow.' It wasn't a question.

'He's here with his father. They have money—' She came to an abrupt stop, her throat working.

'So do I.'

She gave him a tiny smile but he wasn't joking. They wanted to play powerful and well connected? He was brought up to play that game.

'Byron's father thought that I, well, it doesn't matter now, but we don't have the best relationship.' She twisted her bangle round. 'I wanted to be strong enough to do it alone.'

Raff's heart squeezed, painfully. It couldn't be easy for her to ask for help. 'Is Summer going?'

She shook her head. 'They don't want her there.'

'Of course I'll be there.' It was just returning a favour, right? The cold, still anger that consumed him when he saw the stricken look in her eyes, heard her voice shake, watched her search for words no mother should have to say had nothing to do with his decision. It was just a favour. No big deal.

'I've been dreading this,' she confessed, the shadows under her eyes making them look even bigger than usual. 'All I've ever wanted is for Byron to be part of Summer's life. And now he's finally here, in London, just an hour away from her, I'm terrified.' She shook her head helplessly. 'I don't know why. I should be stronger than this.'

Raff stopped and turned her around to face him, tilting her chin up, making her look at him, see the truth of his words. 'Clara, you are incredible. You raise Summer alone, you run a business, half of Hopeford relies on you one way or another. You are the strongest woman I know.'

She stared up at him, doubt in her eyes. 'Really?'

'Really.' He squeezed her shoulders, ignoring the urge to pull her in a little closer.

She exhaled. 'Thank you, I appreciate it. I really do.'

Raff knew instinctively that it wasn't easy for her to lean on him; he was honoured, of course, that she had asked him, had confessed her fears to him. It must have hurt her to show him the vulnerable side she kept so locked away. But it was terrifying as well. Physical intimacy was one thing, emotional intimacy, honesty, secrets? Another ballgame altogether.

But she'd been let down enough already. One morning, that was all she was asking. He was capable of that at least.

As they approached the hotel Clara's demeanour subtly changed, as if she were going into battle. There was little outward sign of her stress although her grip tightened on his arm. Her face was utterly calm as if she were going to any business meeting, her hair had been ruthlessly tamed and coiled back in a neat bun, not one curly tendril allowed to fall about her face. It made her eyes look even bigger, emphasised the catlike curve of her cheek; Raff thought she looked vulnerable, a child playing dress up.

She had dressed for battle too, sleek and purposeful in a grey suit.

But Raff could feel the faint tremors running through her body. Her lips were colourless under her lip gloss.

The Drewes were staying at one of the most exclusive hotels in London, an old Georgian town house discreetly tucked away in a square in Marylebone. It was an interesting choice. Not overtly glitzy but it suggested old money, power and taste.

Raff was looking forward to this. He knew all about old money, power and taste. Bring it on.

Clara was all purpose now, marching up the stone steps and through the double doors, turning with no hesitation towards the hotel's sunny dining room.

'Clara.' Both men rose to their feet; although they both wore smiles the brown eyes were alike—cold and assessing.

'Byron, Mr Drewe.' She shook hands in turn, strangely formal considering one of these men was the father of her child. 'This is Raff.' She didn't qualify their relationship. *Good girl,* Raff thought, *keep them guessing.* 'Raff, this is Byron and his father, Archibald Drewe.'

Raff reached over to shake hands in his turn, unable to resist making his own handshake as strong and powerful as he could. So this was Summer's father, this tall, handsome man, whose smile didn't reach his eyes and who wore his privilege with ease.

'Please, sit down.' The elder Drewe looked very similar to his son, the dark hair almost fully grey and the tanned face more wrinkled but with a steely determination behind the affable façade.

Raff pulled out Clara's chair for her, a statement of intent.

'It's been a while,' she said to Byron. 'You've cut your hair.'

'You look great.' The other man was looking at her with open admiration. 'Haven't changed a bit even if you have changed the sarong for a suit.'

He had seen Clara in a sarong. The hot jealousy that burned through Raff at Byron Drewe's words shocked him. Of course he had seen Clara in a sarong—and a lot less too. He was her ex-lover, the father of her child. At some point Clara had been enamoured enough with this guy to have a baby with him.

And at some point he had allowed her to come home, alone. To raise their child alone.

The jealousy ebbed away, replaced with cold dislike and even colder contempt. 'I am trying to persuade her to link her business with mine. But you know Clara.' He smiled at her. 'She has to be in control. Even a name like Rafferty's doesn't reassure her!'

'Rafferty's?' The older man's eyes were now assessing Raff. 'Impressive.'

The contempt deepened. Now they knew who he was his stock had gone up. Raff hated that.

'What do you do now, Clara?' Should Byron Drewe be smiling at her in that intimate way? Raff allowed himself a brief, self-indulgent fantasy of leaning across the table and planting one perfect punch on that perfect nose.

'I run a concierge service.'

'Half of Hopeford couldn't manage without her, including me,' Raff said.

'How interesting.' The older Mr Drewe couldn't sound less interested. Maybe it was his nose that Raff should fantasise about punching.

'It keeps me busy.' If Clara had heard the snub she wasn't reacting. 'And it's thriving. Between work and Summer I don't have much free time.'

Raff bit back a smile as he mentally applauded. *Nicely done, Clara. Remind them why we're here, ignore their put-downs and make sure they realise you're doing them a favour.*

She didn't need him to step in at all. He might as well help himself to the coffee and sit back and enjoy the show.

'And how is Summer?'

Surely Summer's own grandfather shouldn't pronounce her name in that slightly doubtful way, as if he wasn't quite sure it was right.

Or maybe he just didn't like the name. Clara could scrape her hair back and put on a suit but she knew full well that Archibald Drewe still thought of her a teenage hippy with long hair, tie-dye dresses and a happy-go-lucky attitude who had named her daughter accordingly.

She had been that girl once, but it was a long time ago.

'She's good.' Clara pulled out her tablet. 'I have pictures.'

'That won't be necessary, thank you.'

Time stopped for a long moment, the blood freezing in her veins. How could he dismiss her daughter, his own flesh and blood, in that cold, cavalier way?

'She has your hair, your eyes.' She looked directly at Byron, willing him to stand up for her, for his daughter, for once in his pampered life. 'If you ever look at the pictures I send you you'll know that.'

'I look.' He had the grace to sound ashamed. 'She's beautiful.'

'She is, but she is also smart and kind and very funny. You'd like her.'

He shifted in his seat, evidently uncomfortable. Beside her Raff was leaning back, ostensibly totally at his ease, sipping a cup of coffee. But the set of his shoulders, the line of his jaw told her that he was utterly alert, following every word, every intonation.

Every put-down.

Her hands tightened on her cup; it had been like a game of chicken, leaving asking him along to the last possible moment, kidding herself that she might be able to do this alone. Afraid that his presence might make the whole, nasty situation even more humiliating. She'd thought she'd be ashamed, for him to see this side of her. The dismissed, 'unwanted single mother' side. But having him next to her filled her with the strength she needed to battle on. After all, he had his demons too.

She reached over and laid her hand on his forearm, squeezing very slightly, letting his warmth fill her as she lifted her head and stared evenly at her daughter's father.

'I haven't told her you're here but I hope you have got time to meet her.' She wanted to keep it businesslike but she couldn't help babbling a little, trying to sell her daughter to the one person who shouldn't need the pitch, the one person who should be in regardless.

'She has a picture of you in her room and I tell her lots of stories about you and about Sydney. She helps me put the photos together every Christmas, chooses the pictures she wants to send you. She would love to meet you.'

'Clara, I…' Was that pity in his eyes or shame? Either way it wasn't what she wanted to see.

'It's just, while you're here…'

'I'm getting married.'

Clara stared at Byron blankly. This was why they wanted to see her? Did they think she'd be upset after ten years of silence and neglect, that she was so pathetic she still harboured hopes that they would be a family?

The ego of him.

Raff moved his arm so that his hand lay over hers, lacing his fingers through her fingers, a tacit show of support. She should be annoyed at this overt display of ownership but relief tingled through her instead. 'That's great,' she said, injecting as much sincerity into her voice as she could. 'Congratulations, I hope you'll be very happy.'

'He's marrying Julia Greenwood.'

Archibald Drewe obviously expected this to mean something.

'Great!'

'She's heiress to a media empire,' he told her, his voice oozing contempt for her obvious ignorance. 'This is a brilliant match for Byron, and for our business.'

Much better than a penniless English teenager. She'd known she was never good enough for Byron's family. Once it would have hurt that he had allowed them to influence their future. Now she simply didn't care.

As long as it didn't affect her daughter.

'We want you to sign this.' Archibald Drewe slid a sheaf of papers over the table. Aha, this was the real reason for the meeting. Business, the family way.

'What is it?' Clara made no move to take it.

'Byron is about to join together two great businesses, and any children he and Julia will have…' the emphasis here was intentional '…will inherit a very influential business indeed. We don't want anything from Byron's past to jeopardise his future.'

Anything? They meant anyone.

Beside her Raff was rigid, his hand heavy on hers, fingers digging in, almost painfully.

'And what does this have to do with me?'

'I want to make it quite clear...' Archibald Drewe leant forward; obviously the kid gloves were off '...that your daughter has no claim on me, my son or our business. No claim at all. However...' his smile was as insincere as his eyes were hard '...we are not unfeeling. It's not the girl's fault her beginnings were so unorthodox.'

Raff's arm twitched under hers, the only sign he was alive. Otherwise he was completely still. She couldn't look at him, afraid of what might be in his face. She didn't need his anger and she really couldn't handle pity right now.

The room seemed to have got very cold. She knew how Archibald Drewe felt about her; he had made it completely clear ten years ago. She hadn't expected time to soften him; only money and influence could do that.

But, fool that she was, she hadn't expected him to try and wipe his granddaughter out of the family history books.

'We will send no more annual cheques and you will stop with the photos and emails. Julia does not know of your daughter's existence and neither Byron or I wish her to know. If you sign this contract, however, I will give you a one-off payment of one million pounds sterling in complete settlement of your daughter's claim.'

Raff had met people like the Drewes far too many times; with them it always came down to money. What a cold existence they must lead.

'What does the contract say?' Clara's voice was completely still but she was gripping his hand as if he were the only thing anchoring her.

'It says your daughter has no claim now or in the future on our money or any of our business interests. It also states clearly that she may make no attempts to contact Byron or any member of his family.'

'I see.'

'It's a good offer, Clara.' At least Byron didn't try to meet her eye. Coward.

He had promised himself that he wouldn't intercede but it was no good. How dared they treat Clara like this? 'I'll get my lawyer to have a look at it. Clara isn't signing anything today.' Raff made no attempt to keep the contempt out of his voice.

'That won't be necessary.' Clara pushed the contract away and rose to her feet. 'I won't sign away my daughter's right to contact her father or siblings although don't worry, Byron, I'll do my best to talk her out of it. I would hate for her to be humiliated the way I have been today.'

She was amazing. Calm, clear, holding her anger at bay. But it was costing her; he could hear the strain in her voice, see it in the tense way she stood. What if she hadn't asked him to be there, had had to face these two men alone? It wasn't that she couldn't defend herself. She obviously could. No damsel in distress, this lady. But she shouldn't have to.

She should never have been put into this position. They thought their money and influence gave them the right to treat people like dirt. They were everything he despised.

Raff stood up, taking Clara's hand in his as she continued, her eyes as cold as her voice, but he could feel her hand shaking slightly as she held herself together. 'I won't promise not to send you yearly updates—you don't have to open them but she is your daughter and the least you can do is acknowledge that she exists. As for the money, keep it. I work hard and I provide for her. I always have. I've put every cheque you sent away for her future and that's where it stays. I don't need anything from you, Byron, not any more, and I certainly don't need anything from you, Mr Drewe.'

The older man's face was choleric. 'Now don't be so hasty…'

'If you change your mind, if you want to meet her, then you know where I am. Ready, Raff?'

'Ready.' He got to his feet and nodded at the two men. 'I wish I could say it's been a pleasure but I was brought up to be honest.'

It wasn't until they got outside that Clara realised that she was shaking, every nerve jangling, every muscle trembling.

'Come on.' Raff's eyes were still blazing. 'You've had a shock and you need something to eat. And if I stay anywhere near here I will march back in there and tell them exactly what I think of them.'

'They wouldn't care.' She wasn't just shaking, she was cold to the bone. Clara wrapped her arms around herself trying to get some heat into her frozen limbs.

'I'd feel better though.' He shot her a concerned glance. 'Come here.' He pulled Clara into his embrace, wrapping his arms around her, pressing her close. 'You're like ice.'

She had tried so hard to avoid his touch since that afternoon, since she had let down her guard, but the memory of his touch was seared onto her nerve endings and her treacherous body sank thankfully against him.

'Let's get a taxi. We can go to Rafferty's, get you fed.'

'No, honestly.' Clara wasn't ready to face the world yet. 'Let's just walk. I need some air.'

'Whatever you want.' But he didn't let go of her, not fully, capturing her hands in his, keeping her close as they walked. 'I am going to insist on tea full of sugar though. I work in a medical capacity, remember? I am fully qualified to prescribe hot, sweet drinks.'

Clara knew that if she spoke, just one word, she'd start to cry. And she didn't know if she would ever be able to stop. So she simply nodded and allowed him to continue to hold her hands as they ambled slowly through the grey streets.

'You must think I'm a fool,' she said finally. They had continued to wander aimlessly until they had reached Regent's Park. Raff had bought them both hot drinks from a kiosk and they walked along the tree-lined paths in silence.

Raff looked at her in surprise. 'I don't think anything of the sort. Why?'

'Byron.'

He huffed out a laugh. 'If you judged me on my taste in women when I was eighteen your opinion of me would be very low indeed.'

But Clara didn't want absolution. The humiliation cut so deep. 'I thought I was so worldly. I had travelled thousands of miles alone, with a ticket I had saved up for. I had amazing A-level results. I had it all. I was an idiot. An immature idiot.'

She risked looking into his face, poised to see contempt or, worse, pity, but all she saw was warm understanding. 'I didn't really date at school. I was so focused on my future, on leaving Hopeford. So when I met Byron…' She shook her head. 'We were in Bali, staying in the same hostel. He was two years older and seemed so mature. I had no idea he was from a wealthy family. He didn't act like it. It was his suggestion we share a house in Sydney and save to go travelling together. It was his own little rebellion against his father's plans.'

'We all have those.' His mouth twisted.

'At least yours involves saving people's lives.' She wasn't ready for absolution. 'Byron was just playing. But

I didn't see it. I fell for him completely. When I found out I was pregnant I was really happy. I thought we really had a future, travelling the world with a baby. God, I was so naïve.' She stopped and scuffed her foot along the floor, as unsettled as a teenager on her very first date. 'Thank you.'

Raff raised his eyebrows in surprise. 'What for?'

'For standing by me, for allowing me to handle it.'

'Well,' he confessed, 'that wasn't easy. I don't usually resort to violence but I had to sit on my hands to keep from throttling Byron's father when he offered you the money.'

'Why do men keep offering me money? First you and now him. Why do some people think that throwing money at things—at *me*—solves their problems?'

To her horror Clara could hear that her voice was shaking and feel the lump in her throat was growing. *Keep it together, Clara,* she told herself, but there were times when will power wasn't enough.

Clara blinked, hard, but it was too late as the threatened tears spilled out in an undignified cascade. She knuckled her eyes furiously, as if she could force them back.

'Because we're fools?' Raff took her hand in his, his fingers drawing caressing circles on her palm. It wasn't the first time he had touched her today but this wasn't comforting; the slow, lazy touch sent shivers shooting up her arm.

'No, don't.' She pulled her treacherous hand away. 'You don't have to be nice to me. This is all a pretence, isn't it?' The only person she could ask to stand by her wasn't really in her life at all. How pathetic was that?

Her throat ached with the effort of keeping back the sobs threatening to erupt in a noisy, undignified mess, the tears continuing to escape as Raff took hold of her, tilting her chin up so she had no choice but to look him in the eyes.

'Not all of it,' he said, his voice hoarse. 'It's not all pretence, Clara. Is it? I know we haven't talked about it, try and pretend it didn't happen, but it felt pretty real to me.'

'That was just sex.' Easy to say but she knew her tone lacked conviction. There was no such thing as just sex for Clara; she hadn't trusted anyone enough to get close enough for 'just sex' since Byron. Just this man, standing right here, looking down at her with the kind of mixture of concern and heat that could take a girl's breath away.

'I'm on your side, Clara. I'm here for you, whatever you need, whatever you want.'

Hope sprang up, unwanted, pathetic, needy; she pushed it ruthlessly away. 'For as long as we have a deal, right?' Was that sarcastic voice really hers?

'For as long as it takes, as long as you need me.' His hands tightened on her shoulders, his eyes dark, intense as if he could bore the truth of his words into her.

And, oh, how she wanted to believe him. She didn't mean to move but somehow she was moving forward, allowing herself to lean in, rest her head against the broad shoulders, allowing those strong arms to encircle her, pull her close as the desperate sobs finally overwhelmed her, muffled against his jacket. And he didn't move, just held her tight, let her cry it all out. For as long as she needed to.

CHAPTER EIGHT

'You look…' Raff came to a nonplussed stop, trying to find a word, any word, that did Clara justice. It didn't exist.

'Beautiful?' Clara supplied for him. That wasn't the word; it wasn't enough by any measure. 'I hope so. I've spent all day being prodded, plucked and anointed. If I don't look halfway decent at this exact moment in time then there is no hope.'

'Don't worry,' he assured her. 'You're somewhere past halfway.'

The truth was that at the sight of her all the breath whooshed out of his body; in a room full of glitter she shone the brightest. In the end she had eschewed all the designer dresses Rafferty's had to offer and had opted for a vintage dress that had belonged to her great-grandmother, a ballerina-length full-skirted black silk with a deceptively demure neckline, although it plunged more daringly at the back, exposing a deep vee of creamy skin.

Raff immediately vowed that nobody else would dance with Clara that evening, no other man would be able to put his hand on that bare back, feel the silk of her skin.

'You scrub up nicely as well,' she assured him.

Raff pulled at his bow tie. He'd owned a tux since

his teens but he still felt as if he were dressing up as James Bond.

Or a waiter.

'Nervous?'

'A little,' he admitted. 'Not about the presentation, more how Grandfather will take it. How is he?'

'He's here.' She pulled an expressive face. Her relationship with Raff's grandfather had thawed a little; he was at least polite. But although she told Raff—and herself—that his initial rebuff didn't worry her, she wasn't being entirely honest. It was all too reminiscent of Archibald Drewe's treatment of her, an uneasy and constant reminder of her mistakes.

'Grumpy that he has a special diet and can only drink water but happy he's away from that damned TV and fool nurse. His words not mine.'

'I bet he's glad to be talking work as well.' Raff had mingled business with business and invited some of Rafferty's key suppliers and associates to fill the table he had paid for. It was odd seeing his two very different worlds colliding in this rarefied atmosphere of luxury and wealth.

Opting for something a little unusual, Doctors Everywhere were holding the event in a private garden belonging to the privileged residents of a west London square.

'It's amazing, like a fairy tale.' Clara was looking out at the candlelit gardens, her green eyes shining. Watching the lights play on her hair and face, Raff could only agree.

'We have some very generous—and very rich—patrons,' he said, trying to drag his thoughts back to the business at hand. 'I hadn't even thought about this side of our work. I spend the money, not raise it. I need to talk to Grandfather about allowing them to use Rafferty's for something in the future. We could certainly donate food and staff or raffle prizes.'

And the people he knew could give even more. Helping with the last stages of the fundraiser had been an eye-opener, just not a particularly welcome one.

Raff knew he did a good job out in the field, but anyone with a good grasp of electrics, mechanics and project management could do that. He had other uses that were far more unique: entrée into some of England's richest and most influential echelons and, although he himself didn't value those connections, he knew that no charity could run on good intentions alone. Ensuring the donations came in was a vital role.

But would it be as satisfying? Or would it be a gilded cage just like the one he was working so hard to escape from?

'Is everything set up?' Clara was as cool and collected as ever, on the surface at least, but when he took her arm he felt the telltale tremble.

'Ready to go,' he promised her. 'My mission tonight is to get all these people to remember why they're here and part with as much money as possible.'

And throw the gauntlet down. Show his grandfather that this was where he belonged—and this was where he was staying, no matter what. Only he didn't feel the same burning need to get back out into the field. It helped, of course, that he had been helping to set up the fundraiser, interacting with colleagues, seeing a new side of the charity's work. But it was more than that.

Clara. Everything he didn't want or need in his life. She needed stability and commitment and a father for her daughter, not a travelling jack of all trades whose idea of a perfect day with family meant a day by himself. And yet, and yet…

Somehow she had got under his skin. More than attraction, more than lust. He respected her, admired her strength—but it was those glimpses of carefully hidden vulnerability that really hooked him in. He knew how much she hid it, despised any display of weakness. But she had trusted him enough to lean on him, cry on him, allow him to shoulder her burdens for a short time.

From Clara that was a rare and precious gift. But was he worthy? And was he capable of accepting all that she had to offer?

'They certainly do a lot of good.' Raff's grandfather had been slowly softening throughout the evening, his initial scepticism disappearing when he saw his table companions and the carefully prepared meal that had been specially provided for him. If he still cast a longing look or two at the bottles of very expensive wine that littered the table, he had at least stopped complaining and was sipping the despised mineral water with martyred compliance.

'I had no idea about the sheer scale of their work,' Clara agreed. 'Nor just how desperate things can be. I'll never complain about waiting for a doctor's appointment again.'

Raff and his colleagues spent their lives making sure that people all over the globe, people who lived in poverty, who had fled their homes, who had seen their world turned into warzones still had access to medicine, to doctors. To hope.

He could have taken the easy option, the job provided for him, the family money, enjoyed all that London had to offer the young and the rich. In a way she wished he had; it would be so easy to keep her distance from that man. Much harder to stay away from the man sitting next to her, even though there was no way there could ever be any kind of happy ever after between them.

But in the few days since the meeting with Byron something had changed. They were easier with each other, more intimate. Hands brushed, lingered, eyes met, held. Nothing had happened, not again, but the promise of it hung seductively over them.

Butterflies tumbled around her stomach, a warm tingle spreading through her at the thought.

'I'm sorry.' Raff finally managed to gracefully extricate himself from the conversation he was embroiled in. 'I've been neglecting you all evening.'

'That's okay.' After all, she was being paid for her time.

Not that Clara felt she could charge a penny for tonight; she would ask Raff to donate her fee back to the charity.

Raff pulled a face. 'I'd much rather be talking to you, but I have been promising myself that as soon as the dancing starts I am all yours.' His eyes were full of promise and a shiver ran through her despite the heat in the overcrowded room.

'You didn't say anything about dancing,' Clara protested. 'I can barely walk in these heels, let alone dance.'

'Don't worry.' His expression was pure wicked intent. 'I won't let you fall.'

'You better not. When are you on?'

'In a few minutes. Wish me luck?'

Clara put one hand on his cheek, allowing herself the luxury of touch, rubbing her palm along the rough stubble. 'Good luck,' but she knew he didn't need it. If he managed to get one hundredth of his charm across then he would have the guests clamouring to outbid each other.

The presentations had been spread out throughout the evening. A welcome speech before canapés, then, after the starters, two of the nurses gave an evocative talk that brought their exciting, dangerous and very necessary work alive. A surgeon's visceral yet compelling description of the challenges she faced was an uneasy filler between the main course and pudding.

No one else seemed to notice the incongruity between their surroundings, with the conspicuous display of wealth and luxury, and the poverty and need so eloquently conveyed. Clara saw women wiping tears, the diamonds on their hands and wrists worth more than the total the charity was trying to raise.

'We need to make sure everyone is suitably worked up before the auction,' Raff whispered. 'They'll all be well fed and watered. We want them to go home with their consciences as sated as their stomachs!'

Just the nearness of him, though he was barely touching her, that lightest of contact, sent tremors rippling up and down her body. For so long she had been shut away in a box of her own design, not allowing herself to do or to feel. Constraining herself to the narrowest of lives. And it had worked. She hadn't been hurt, hadn't messed up.

But she hadn't felt either. Hadn't felt this bitter-sweetness ache. That awareness that overtook everything so that all she could see was him; she could feel nothing but his breath on her cheek, sending waves of need shuddering through her.

Clara took a deep breath, trying to regulate her hammering pulse, remember where they were, what he was about to do. 'So it's up to you to seal the deal?'

He grimaced. 'I wish they'd put me on first. Logistics isn't exactly the sexiest subject. They'll be eying up the petits fours and coffee and be in a post-dinner slump by the time the auction comes around.'

'Don't be ridiculous.' Clara reached for his hand and squeezed it, trying to quell the absurd jump every nerve gave as her fingers tangled with his. 'If anybody can make logistics fascinating, you can. Go get them.'

Raff turned and looked at her and for one long moment the tent fell away, the people fading away to nothing but a murmuring backdrop to the scorching intensity of his gaze. 'You think?'

'I do.' And she did. This was a new side to the confident, nonchalant playboy—but then wasn't that playboy just a façade? A mask he wore well but a mask nonetheless. And the more Clara saw the passionate, principled man behind it, the more she wanted to retreat, to run away.

She'd thought playboys were her downfall. She'd been wrong. She had survived Byron, left him with her head held high and her heart only slightly cracked. But a man who cared, a man who carried the weight of the world on his broad shoulders? That was a far scarier prospect.

'I think you can do anything,' she said. 'Including make every person here spend three times more than they budgeted for.'

'That's my aim.' The words were jokey but his face was deadly serious. 'Ready to clap nice and loudly?'

'That's my job.'

'I'll make sure I give you a good reference.'

Was it her imagination or did disappointment pass fleetingly over his face at her words? That would be ridiculous, Clara told herself sternly. They both knew what this was. This was a business arrangement. A glitzy, intimate contract maybe but a contract nonetheless. Money was changing hands, favours were being done. That was all.

'Okay, then.' And he was gone, the eyes of half the women in the room following the tall figure as he strode across the marquee.

Clara sank back in her chair, an unaccountable feeling of melancholy passing over her. What had he wanted her to say? She didn't know; she was no good at this. Had swapped flirting for nappies and never quite got her groove back.

'This means a lot to him.'

She jumped. For a moment she'd forgotten where she was, that she was surrounded by people. 'I'm sorry?'

Charles Rafferty was looking up at the stage where his grandson stood, talking to the computer technician. Raff was relaxed, laughing, totally at home.

'I knew he had this ridiculous hankering to be a doctor—it was because of his father's illness, of course, that's why I persuaded him to switch to business; besides, I needed him. But his heart was never in it. When he said he was off to work for these people I thought that a bit of time and freedom would sort him out. That he'd come back to me.'

She had no idea what to say.

Raff was responsible for people's lives every day. He didn't cut them open, administer the medicine, nurse them, but he made that possible. He worked in impossible conditions in impossible countries for an impossibly tiny wage.

And he loved it. It was good that his grandfather was seeing that, acknowledging it.

'He doesn't want to let you down,' she said, aware what a lame response it was.

'No.' The older man looked at her, really looked at her

for the first time in the weeks since they had met. And for once there was no trace of a sneer on his face. Just hollow loss. 'He's aware of his family responsibilities. I made sure of that. He was only eight when his father had the stroke, when it was obvious his father would never recover. Only eight when I anointed him as my heir.'

'And Polly?' Okay, she was going beyond anywhere she had any right to go. But Polly was her friend. And Raff? He meant something to her, something a little like friendship.

'Polly?' He shook his head. 'I made a mess of it, didn't I? I inherited the company from my father and groomed my son to take my place with Castor waiting in the wings. It didn't even occur to me that he might not want it—or that Polly did.'

'Look, he's ready.' Raff had stepped up onto the temporary stage and was gesturing for quiet. He dominated the marquee, tall, imposing, his sheer force of will stopping the chatter as people turned to listen. 'I'm sure you'll work it out,' she said quietly as the main light dimmed, leaving just one spotlight trained directly onto Raff.

The silence was expectant. Clara was aware of nothing but the ache of anticipation twisting her stomach. *Do well,* she urged him silently. *Make them see.* Looking at her hands, she was surprised to see her nails digging into her palms. She didn't feel any pain but when she unfurled her hands there were crescent marks embedded in the soft skin. When had he started to matter so much? When had she begun to care?

It wasn't just because she had helped him, gone over the presentation over and over until it made no sense to either of them.

'I know you are all ready for your coffees.' Raff hadn't raised his voice at all yet every syllable carried to every corner. 'And listening to me talk about project management isn't going to raise your heart rate the way my very talented colleagues did. I have watched them perform surgeries, vaccinate children and deliver babies in every kind of condition you can think of—and I was still blown away by their talks earlier. So no, I can't compete with them. My job now, as in the field, is to enable their work. And this, ladies and gentleman, is how I do it.'

He raised a hand and pressed a button and immediately the room was filled with the sound of drums building up into a crescendo as the screen behind him burst into life.

Raff had elected not to go for a talk and slides, knowing that the previous presentations would be using photos to great effect. Instead he had put together a video, a montage of photos and film showing a 'typical' day in his life, backdropped by fast, evocative music. The film started by panning around a small dorm room, ending in a different if similar room, and took in five different clinics and hospitals, two camps and four temporary clinics during the ten-minute show.

Raff was shown sitting in an office with paperwork piled on top of a crowded desk, spanner in hand, eying up a battered old truck, in a helicopter, setting up a tent, fixing a tap, spade in hand digging a pit, playing volleyball outside a tent, watching a spectacular desert sunset.

But the main focus of the film was the patients and people using the facilities he built, repaired and managed.

As the camera lingered on a queue of women waiting patiently to vaccinate their children, he spoke. 'We need running water, toilets, moving vehicles, electricity, satellite connections, working kitchens, working sterilisers for the most basic of our clinics. The hospitals are a whole other level. It all needs to be brought in on budget and just to add to my woes our staff and volunteers quite like to be fed, have somewhere to sleep and the chance to get to the nearest city to enjoy their time off. It's exhausting, often sweaty and dirty, and involves spreadsheets, but on the rare occasion when everything is working I can stand back and I see this.'

Another image flashed up and stayed there. A small boy beaming at the camera, one leg wrapped in bandages, his arm encased in plaster. 'I see children with a future, families kept together, mothers who will live to watch their children grow up. I see hope.

'Thanks to you we will be able to keep vaccinating, operating, delivering and curing. Your generous donations mean that children, just like Matthew here, have a future. Thank you. I'm now going to give you the opportunity to show just how generous you can be. There are some fabulous prizes in our auction. Dig deep, dig hard and bid as high as you can.'

The spotlight dimmed and the house lights were switched back on as the room erupted into applause. People were on their feet congratulating Raff as he walked around the room.

'That was different,' Charles Rafferty said drily. But, Clara noted, his eyes were moist.

'It was good, wasn't it?' she agreed. 'Luckily Raff blogs a lot when he's out in the field and often embeds video or pictures so he had a lot of footage he could use.'

'If he goes back,' Raff's grandfather said, his eyes fixed on Clara, the intent gaze eerily similar to that of his grandson, 'what about you?'

Clara's mouth dried. She had kind of got used to having him around, sitting on her desk disrupting her, whispering highly libellous biographies of the people they met, raising an approving eyebrow as she made small talk.

She had got used to those moments when their hands brushed, the sensation that time was slowing and that all she could see or hear was him. The swell that seemed to roar upwards, filling her full of awareness of his every movement, his every gesture.

'We've managed so far,' she said as lightly as she could. 'Skype, letters, it works really well. We're both so busy that time apart gives us a chance to breathe. Excuse me for a moment.'

The tent seemed so bright, so loud. The chatter and the music competing with each other, driving up the noise level to a deafening shriek. Each of the myriad lights seemed to shine directly into her eyes, the heat making her stomach roll. She needed air and quiet and dark. She needed some space.

Clara moved quickly across the tent, swerving to avoid the clustered groups, making sure she didn't catch anyone's eye as the announcer returned to the stage to announce the start of the auction. Thankfully, she reached the marquee entrance and slipped out into the grounds.

What was wrong with her? It had been a highly successful night. Raff's presentation had been sensational, the guests all looked ready to start spending and donating lavishly and if Clara had read him correctly then Raff's grandfather looked ready to do the right thing and give the company to Polly.

Even better, she had made some great contacts and, if she dared, was in a great position to expand out of Hopeford.

If she dared. Was that it? Was that the reason for this melancholy that had fallen on her like a damp dusk? Because starting the business had been absurdly simple; it had all fallen into place with surprising ease. But taking it into the big city meant taking risks and that was something Clara just didn't do any more.

Or was it because this adventure was nearly over? She'd thought that she was finished with adventures but maybe that part of her wasn't as dead and buried as she liked to think. As she had hoped. Compared to backpacking around the world it was a tame adventure, true, but a part of her was thrilling to the unpredictability.

And Raff. Clara sighed, feeling the truth exhale out of her with her heavy breath. There it was. Like a fool she was allowing the pretence to take over. Just because they pretended it was a relationship, acted as if it were a relationship, did not make it one. He didn't want or need ties here; he was doing his best to sever the ones he already had.

There was nothing long term for her. She should be sensible. Just as she always was.

'Here you are.' Clara's heart gave an absurd skip at the low voice; clearly the sensible memo hadn't reached it yet. 'Are you okay?'

'A little hot.' That wasn't a lie. 'Shouldn't you be inside for the auction?'

'There's not much call for exotic villas or cases of fine wine out in the field,' he said, walking up behind her and wrapping his arms around her. All thoughts of caution, of taking a step back, fled at his touch. 'I did purchase an obscene amount of raffle tickets, though. You?'

'I don't think there's any point in me competing against any of those platinum cards.' There had been some amazing items on the auction list but the guide prices alone had made Clara take a hasty gulp of her wine. 'I think your grandfather was planning to bid. Maybe we should go back in.'

'He's quite capable of spending a lot of money without

my help.' Raff's arms tightened a little, his breath hot on her neck, burning her, branding her, sending heat flaming through her veins. 'I'm looking forward to spending some time off duty.' He turned her unresisting body round, cupping her face with his hand. 'I just want a night with no more work talk, a beautiful woman on my arm, in my arms. Music, wine, fun. Are you in? Because…' his voice was low, intimate '…there's no one else I want to be with.'

She had spent the last ten years building up a reputation, one she was proud of. She was often called driven, reliable, honest—and she was proud of those attributes. But beautiful? Fun?

Raff thought she was both of them. And tonight, just tonight, Clara thought she might think so too.

'Just one night?' That was what he had said, right? Was it enough? It had to be.

'Is that all you want?'

'Yes.' That was the right answer, wasn't it? She searched his face for answers but he was giving nothing away. Only his eyes showed any expression: heat, want, need. What was she waiting for? 'No. I don't know. You're going away.'

'I work away,' he corrected her.

She stared at him, confused. 'What are you saying?'

He smiled at her, dangerous and sweet. 'I'm saying there's no need to plan ahead.' His hand slid down her shoulder, moved to caress the exposed skin on her back.

Clara felt her stomach drop, her knees literally weaken; she had never realised that could actually happen in real life. Any second now she was going to have to grab hold of him just to keep herself upright.

'Chemistry like this doesn't come along often…' his hand was drifting up and down, scorching a blazing trail along her spine '…but it's more than chemistry. I like you, Clara. A lot. I like how we are together. I like who I am when I'm with you. I think we should stop fighting it and go with it.' He paused, his gaze moving down to linger on her mouth. 'See where it takes us.'

See where it takes us. Somewhere new, somewhere dangerous. But there had been a flash of something in his eyes when he said he liked her. Something heartfelt.

And she liked him too. More than she wanted to admit to herself. He didn't fit any of the criteria she had painstakingly typed into the internet dating sites. He wasn't local, didn't have a steady job, wasn't family orientated. But he made her laugh, made her feel safe—and he made her tremble with need.

Was that enough?

She was over-thinking it. She had said she wanted to try dating again and here was this gorgeous man ready and waiting.

Waiting for her to say yes.

She had to say yes. Raff had never before put himself on the line like that, not for anybody. He didn't know what would happen when he was back out in the field, where they would be this time next year, but he didn't care. Even the thought that they might *be* somewhere next year didn't trigger his usual flight reflexes.

Slowly, his eyes on hers, searching for consent, he reached out and trailed a finger along the feline curve of her cheek, down to her full bottom lip. She stared up at him, eyes wide, endlessly green, questioning.

Whatever she was asking he obviously supplied the right answer because she moved. One small step closer, bringing her full body into contact with his. Raff moved his finger, reluctantly, off the smooth, full lip and followed the curve of her jaw, her skin silky under his touch.

He reached the tip of that pointed little chin and slid his finger under, tilting her face up towards him.

He waited for one torturous second, giving her plenty of time to change her mind before allowing himself to dip his head towards hers for a soft, barely there, sweet leisurely kiss, her mouth opened under his, soft, yielding.

'What do you say, Clara?' he whispered against her mouth. 'Will you come back with me tonight? Come back with me now?'

She leant in and claimed his mouth with hers. 'Yes,' she whispered back. 'I say yes.'

CHAPTER NINE

'I SHOULD HAVE KNOWN I'd find you here. Afraid you'd turn into a pumpkin if you didn't get home before sunrise?' Was that anger in his voice? Clara swallowed, reaching for the hole punch on her desk, settling it back into a perfect line.

'I didn't want anyone to see me leaving.' She couldn't meet his eyes as she answered him. It was the truth, but only half the truth.

She had woken up in the early hours, nestled in his arms, and for one blissful moment had felt happy, sated. Safe. Tempted to wake him up to see if it could be as magical a third or fourth time.

And then reality intruded. How could she face the next morning? The intimacy of early morning conversation, coffee, breakfast—followed by the walk of shame in strappy heels and yesterday's dress. She wasn't sure which scared her more.

She didn't want to be that woman, sneaking out of a bedroom in the dark, shoes in one hand, balled up tights in the other, and yet somehow there she was, tiptoeing through the dark streets until she reached the sanctuary of home and a sleepless night alone in her own cold and empty bed.

'I didn't think you'd mind,' she said in the end. 'I

mean, it's midday and you've only just turned up.' She wanted to recall the words as soon as she'd said them. She didn't want him to know that she'd been watching the door, her phone, her email, half desperately hoping that he would be doing his utmost to track her down.

Half hoping he'd stay well away.

His eyes narrowed. 'I didn't think you were the kind of woman to play games, Clara.'

Ouch. 'I'm not.' Not usually anyway. 'But last night was…' amazing, magical, the best night of her life '…like a fairy tale. I wasn't sure either of us knew what we were doing. Not really.'

They'd spent so much time together, shared so many secrets, danced around the attraction they felt for so long, it was easy to be swept up in the romance. The thought of waking up to regret and apology on his face—or conversely to expectation and hope—was more than she could bear. Far better to run.

She'd never thought of herself as a coward before.

'I knew exactly what I was doing,' he said silkily and she flushed at the sarcastic tone. 'I thought I made it very clear to you that I was in this. With you. But if you can't trust me then there's not really any point, is there?'

'I do trust you.' It was herself she didn't trust; she had got it so very wrong before.

He laughed, a short, hard sound, running his hand through his hair as he shook his head. 'You won't let me in, Clara. You don't want people around here to see us together, to know you stayed over. I haven't met your parents or your daughter. Seriously, when I said I was in, it wasn't as your bit on the side.'

'That isn't fair.' Clara jumped up, sending her chair skittering backwards. 'You told me you liked me yesterday. Yesterday! What does that mean, anyway? We're not in school any more.'

'No, that's why I thought we could try and have an adult relationship.' He sighed. 'Come on, Clara, what do you want? I'm not the kind of guy to offer you hearts and flowers and big romantic gestures. This is new to me too. I thought we could take it one day at a time, find our way into this thing. But if you won't let me in then there's no way it's ever going to work.'

Feel our way in? One day at a time? It was hardly a grand declaration but it was the best he had. Raff wanted this thing, whatever it was, to be honest from the start. His father had treated his mother like a princess, splurged expensive gifts and holidays on her, never allowed her to shoulder a single responsibility. And then the second she had needed to step up she had disintegrated. If Raff was going to try something more serious than a simple fling then it had to be equal.

And that meant honesty.

Damn, he knew relationships were hard but he hadn't expected to feel as bereft as he had this morning. Waking up to find her side of the bed empty, her clothes gone. If it weren't for the faint scent of her perfume in the air he would have thought he had imagined the whole thing.

'I do want to let you in.' She was still standing behind her desk, a physical as well as an emotional barrier between them. 'I'm just not sure how. My parents, Summer, I don't want to let them down again.'

'You think I'll let them down?' Was that really her opinion of him?

'You said yourself one day at a time. How can I risk my daughter's happiness on that?'

Raff huffed out an exasperated laugh. 'All relation-ships are one day at a time, Clara. Anyone who says oth-erwise is a liar and a fool.'

He took a deep breath, trying to steady his pulse. 'You want to know why I didn't come rushing round here this morning?' Apart from needing time to calm down be-fore facing her. 'I went to visit my grandfather. To tell him that as much as I love him and appreciate him I can't be who he wants me to be, do what he wants me to do.'

'So you are going back?' She wasn't looking at him, straightening the few items on her desk over and over. He wanted to walk over, remove the stapler and ruler and make her listen. Instead he hung back by the door.

'I was always going back.' He had made that clear right from the start, from the first moment of attraction. 'But it's not full time. We are only ever allowed to do short-term contracts. I could be back in the UK for four months of the year. I've offered to stay on the board at Rafferty's but that's it.'

It hadn't been easy; his grandfather had known all too well what Raff was going to say and had put up some resistance—he wouldn't be Charles Rafferty if he didn't—but in the end he had gracefully bowed down to the inevitable.

It had been a massive relief. Raff didn't want to cut all his ties with his family; imperfect and demanding as they were, they were all he had.

But it didn't have to be that way—if Clara would just allow him in, let them try. Four months a year wasn't a huge amount, he knew that. But it was all he had right now. It was a start.

'And Polly?'

'The company's hers, so all we need is the lady her-self. I guess this is when we find out if you've been holding out on me after all.' He meant the words to sound light but they came out dark. Bitter.

Her head shot up. 'Is that what you think?'

'Clara, I don't know what to think.'

She looked stricken, her eyes full of hurt. 'I haven't lied, Raff. All I have is an email address. But she did say to use it if I needed to get in touch so I can send a message letting her know what's happened. If you want me to.'

This could be the moment when he turned around and walked away. He could head back to Jordan completely free. No Rafferty's, no family expectations, no Clara.

Freedom wasn't all it was cracked up to be.

Slowly he moved across the room, his eyes fixed on hers. 'We can do better than this.' His voice was low. 'I wish I could promise you it will all work out but I can't.'

He had reached the side of her desk and held out his hand to her. After a long moment's deliberation she took it, allowing him to draw her out. 'I won't lie to you, Clara. I don't know what's going to happen. And I know four months a year isn't very much. But I think we could be good, if we just tried. If you wanted to.'

'I do want to,' she whispered.

He didn't want to fight with her, didn't want to argue about the future. He just wanted the here and now, to enjoy the present.

He stepped closer, one hand slipping around her waist, the other slipping through the silky tendrils of hair as he finally kissed her good morning. It wasn't the lazy waking-up kiss he had hoped for but right now all he wanted was to taste her, reassure her.

Her mouth was warm and honey sweet; her hands fastened around the nape of his neck, light and cool yet capable of igniting with just one touch. Raff buried one hand in the smooth strands of her hair, anchoring himself to her.

He kept the kiss light, using every ounce of his control to tantalisingly nibble along her bottom lip, resisting her attempts to deepen it, to push it further, harder. Hotter.

His hand splayed out along her waist, tracing the faint outline of her ribs, enjoying knowing that just a couple of inches higher and he would brush against the fullness of her breast, a couple of inches further down and he would brush over the curve of her hips round to her pert bottom. The urge to rush nearly overwhelmed him but he held back with superhuman restraint.

It would be easy, so easy and, oh, so tempting to pick her up, allow those shapely legs to wrap around him, to carry her across the room, lock the door and drop her on one of those plump, inviting sofas.

So tempting. But there was no need to rush. Because part of being an adult meant learning that anticipation was part of the game—and it made the end result all the sweeter.

Slowly, reluctantly, he pulled back. Clara's eyes were glazed, heavy-lidded, her mouth swollen. 'Good morning,' he whispered and was rewarded by a slow, sweet smile.

'Good morning.'

'Shall we start again?'

Her eyes clouded over. It wasn't an encouraging sign. 'Raff...'

Whatever she was going to say was cut short as the front door was flung open, banging against the wall.

Clara jumped back and resumed her official face in less time than it took Raff to register the sound.

'Summer.' She sounded shocked and the look she threw Raff was a mixture of apology and warning. 'What are you doing home?'

Raff turned round and saw a slim girl aged about ten, the pointed chin and high cheekbones clearly marking her kinship to Clara although the dark eyes and hair were her only legacy from her absent father. A stab of anger hit him that Byron had chosen money over fatherhood. The merry-faced girl deserved more.

Every child deserved more.

'Half day.' Summer dropped her satchel onto the sofa. 'Don't you remember?'

'Wasn't Grandma picking you up?' Clara wasn't even looking at him.

'Yes, she dropped me back here though, as I didn't see you yesterday. Who's this?'

Raff watched with interest as the colour rose on Clara's cheeks. 'This is a client of mine…'

'Not any more,' Raff interjected. He smiled at the girl. 'Hi, I'm Raff.'

'Oh.' Summer looked at him with interest. 'The VIC?'

'The what?' Raff didn't spend much time with children. He feared it showed.

'Very Important Client. The reason Mummy has been so busy.'

'That's finished now.' Clara had regained her usual colour. 'Obviously we'll still look after the house but the, er, the project has come to an end. Mr Rafferty has come in to collect his invoice.' She glared meaningfully at Raff.

'And to celebrate.' This was it, the chance to prove to Clara that he was a fit person to be in Summer's life. 'How do you two ladies fancy an afternoon out at Howland Hall?'

'The theme park? Yes, please!'

'I don't think so.'

The two voices spoke at once.

'Mummy, please, I've never been on a roller coaster.' The big eyes turned appealingly to Clara.

'Mr Rafferty, can I just have a quick word?' Clara took Raff's arm and led him to the back of the office, through the French doors and into the courtyard beyond.

'What are you doing?' she snapped. 'This is not okay.'

Unease slithered over him. 'What?'

Clara glared at him. 'Offering to take Summer out.'

He looked at her bemusedly. 'I won a family pass in the raffle last night. I thought it would be nice.'

'You know I don't let Summer meet men I'm dating.' Clara put her hand on her forehead, rubbing distractedly. She looked tired. 'It's not fair on her. What if she gets attached? You're going away.'

'It's an afternoon at a theme park, not an invitation to move in.' What was she getting so worried about? Hang on. 'How many men?'

'What?'

'How many men have you not allowed Summer to meet?' The thought of her out with other men made him lose all focus.

'None yet but there may be. In the future. After all, you said one day at a time…' She didn't finish the sentence; she didn't need to. 'But that's not the point. I don't want Summer going to theme parks and I don't want her going on roller coasters and I don't want her getting attached to you.'

He put his hands on her shoulders. 'Relax, Clara. Every child needs to go on a roller coaster and I promise to be as dull as I can. She'll be so unattached she'll be like a broken jigsaw.'

She chewed her lip. 'I don't know.'

'One afternoon.'

'Roller coasters are dangerous.'

'Not at Howland Hall. They're known for their safety measures. You can't let her grow up without having ever been on a roller coaster. She'll rebel, become a stunt-woman or join the circus. Buy a motorbike for sure.'

'She has promised me she'll never get on a bike!' Clara bit her lip. 'I don't know, Raff.'

'I do,' he said promptly. 'Afternoon of adrenaline-fuelled, gravity-defying fun and then I'll take you both out for dinner somewhere where jeans and trainers are welcomed. If our stomachs can handle it, that is. As a thank-you, to Summer as well. She must have missed you the last few weeks.'

Clara had mentioned that her daughter had found her continued absence difficult; Raff *did* owe her a treat. At least that was what he told himself, pushing away the sudden and unwanted feeling of protectiveness that slammed into him when he thought of her absent father.

Clara twisted the bangle on her wrist round and round, a sure sign she was unsure. 'As long as she knows that's what this is,' she said after a long moment. 'A thank-you. I don't want her getting the wrong idea. And we'll take the van. I'm not letting her into that tiny back seat of yours. I bet it doesn't even have a seat belt.'

'I'll call you Miss Castleton and keep ten metres be-tween us at all times,' Raff promised. 'Now, do you like to be at the front or the back of the roller coaster? The middle is strictly for wimps.'

'This,' Summer said rapturously as she bounced along between Clara and Raff, 'is the best day ever. I only want to do things with VIP tickets, Mummy. It's cool not having to queue.'

'There's nothing wrong with taking your turn,' Clara said, but she didn't even convince herself. Unfair it might be, but there was something to be said for waltzing up to the front of every queue, even though Clara found she couldn't meet the accusing eyes of the people who had been waiting patiently for up to an hour to board one of the world-famous roller coasters.

They had been on the Scorpion twice, Runaway Train three times and the Dragonslayer five times. She'd lost count of how many times they had been on the Rapids. They were all soaked through but luckily as spring slid into summer the weather was complying, and even though she kept checking Summer anxiously her daughter was showing no sign of being chilled.

'I want to go on that one,' Summer said for what must be the twentieth time, pointing over at the Typhoon. Clara shuddered. 'You're too short,' she said firmly.

'I'm not. I'm tall for my age,' Summer insisted.

'Let's go and have a look,' Raff interjected easily. 'There's a height chart just outside and you can have a proper look at it, Summer. You might change your mind when you see how green the people getting off it look.'

It wasn't his place to intercede and part of Clara resented it, but another part of her liked the sharing of the load, the way he interacted with her daughter. The two of them were slightly ahead, strolling along the concrete path. Summer was explaining something involved to Raff, something about roller coasters judging by her expansive hand gestures. It was strange seeing her with a man who wasn't her grandfather, seeing the way she responded to his gentle teasing and laid-back questions.

The old familiar ache twisted around her stomach. She had let Summer down; her daughter needed a father, someone to urge her forward when Clara's instinct was to hold her back, hold her tight.

Raff would be perfect. But would it be fair on Summer when he would be gone so frequently?

Would it be fair to Clara, herself? On the one hand she would keep her independence, wouldn't have to compromise anything in her life. But surely if she was going to take such a big step then there should be some changes.

The theme park was set in the grounds of an old, now abandoned stately home and the owners played up to its heritage. Although there was a vast amount of plastic signage they tried to keep everything vintage-looking; even the food carts and toilets had an Edwardian country-garden look, the staff smart in striped blazers and straw hats,

'It's so cool.' Summer was gazing up at the park's newest ride, her eyes huge. 'Look, Mummy.'

Clara shuddered. 'I feel sick just looking, Sum. How can you want to go on that?' She had never allowed her onto anything faster than a carousel before but there was an adrenaline junkie hidden in her demure daughter. She wanted to try everything.

She reminded Clara of herself when she was young.

'They look like they're flying.'

'If humans were meant to fly, we'd have wings. Honestly, I can cope with any normal roller coaster but this?' The riders were strapped in but their legs were left free, to dangle helplessly as the roller coaster snaked at incredible speed around the twists, turns and loops. That was bad enough but after the first loop the carriages went horizontal, leaving the hapless passengers facing down as the train swooped along the thin rails.

'There's the height sign.' Summer went racing over to it. 'I'm big enough, Mummy, look. Can I go on it, please, please?'

'I don't know.' Her instinct was to say no, just as she

had instinctively wanted to refuse Clara's pleas to go on anything apart from the caterpillar train aimed at the under threes. But she had swallowed down her fears and let her daughter go. And look how happy she was, eyes shining, her face lit up with enthusiasm.

Over the last few weeks it had become painfully apparent just how much she sheltered Summer—and herself—from any kind of physical or mental stress. And that was good, right? Only, maybe, she had crossed the line, just a little, into overprotectiveness.

Better to be overprotective than neglectful. But Summer was growing up, and if she pulled too tightly now she knew it could cause problems later; it was just so hard to let go, even a little.

'I really hate the idea of it, sweetie. I don't think I can.' She'd conquered her own reluctance and gone on every single ride so far, as if sitting by Summer's side would keep her safe, She'd been not so secretly relieved when Summer's age had put a couple of the most terrifying beyond their reach. 'I need to feel something under my feet if I'm travelling at that speed.'

Summer's face fell but she didn't ask again, just nodded in agreement. Despite her good behaviour she couldn't hide her disappointment; her whole body projected it from her drooping shoulders to the tip of her toe scuffing the pavement.

Raff took Clara's arm, pulling her a short distance away, out of Summer's earshot. 'I'll take her on.'

Panic immediately clawed at Clara's chest. 'No, you don't have to.'

He grinned. 'I want to try it. It's meant to be great.'

'You're hanging from a bar looking down at the ground hundreds of feet below and travelling at G-force speeds. How can that be great?'

'Come on, Clara, I know the adrenaline gets you. You're buzzing every time we get off a ride.'

Adrenaline or raw fear? Clara wasn't even sure there was a difference. 'It's not…' She paused. She didn't want to say safe. Not again. Even if every fibre was screaming at her that it wasn't. 'It's not your responsibility.'

'No, but I'm offering. Look, we passed a café just a couple of minutes back up that path. Why don't you go and have a horribly overpriced coffee so you don't even have to watch and we'll find you when we're done?'

'Please, Mummy.' Summer had come dancing over; her eyes pleaded with Clara.

What harm could it do? They had VIP passes so they wouldn't have to join the lengthy queue. In just twenty minutes' time, Summer would be telling her about every twist, turn and scream.

And she would never know that allowing her to go on the ride took far more out of Clara than any roller coaster in the world.

'Okay, then.' She staggered backwards as Summer flung herself onto her with a high-pitched squeal. 'You do everything Raff tells you and remember, if you change your mind just say. No one will be cross or think you're a coward.'

'I won't change my mind. Thank you, Mummy, thank you, Raff. This is totally epic.'

'Totally,' he agreed. 'See you soon, Clara. Enjoy the calm. I think a return to the Rapids after this, don't you? After all, my socks are almost dry now!'

Surely they must be finished now? Clara checked her watch for what felt like the hundredth time. Wanting to block out even the mental image of her daughter queuing and boarding such an unnatural ride, she had opted for a seat at the other side of the café by a large window over-looking a shady pond. Once seated with a latte she had immersed herself in work emails on her mobile. After all, technically it was a work day.

But Sue was proving as ferociously efficient at run-ning the office as she was at running a house and it had only taken Clara twenty minutes to clear the backlog. Without work the old, all-too familiar panic reasserted itself. She swallowed, trying to dislodge the lump in her throat, the clutching sensation at her chest. Summer was fine, she was with Raff, she was on a ride designed to be completely safe despite all outward appearances.

But, oh, if only Summer didn't have to grow up. Maybe the witch in Rapunzel had a point. She was very misunderstood if you ignored the eye-gouging part. In fact, Clara could look up any convenient towers in forests for sale right now and deposit Summer at the top of one.

She sighed. Maybe that was just a little over the top.

Drinking the last bitter, lukewarm dregs, Clara tapped her fingers on the wooden table top. Maybe she should go out there and wait, be at the exit, beaming, ready to welcome her daughter back to solid ground. She needed to hide her fears better, show support for all Summer's whims, schemes and plans just as her parents had for her. Just as they still did.

Mind made up, Clara pushed her chair out and gath-ered up her bag and jacket and the coats Raff and Sum-mer had left with her. Arms full, she walked towards the exit, deliberately keeping her steps unhurried, hoping if she projected an aura of calm she might even come to believe it herself.

It was only an hour until closing time and the café had been quiet, almost eerily so compared with the hustle and bustle outside. The screams of the riders mingled with the cries of the hot and overtired toddlers and babies punctuated by screeches and laughter from the school groups and gangs of older teenagers. The day was still unseasonably warm and the coats were stuffy in her arms as she walked towards the ride.

It was odd how the noise seemed to dim as she approached the area dedicated to Typhoon. No rattle of wheels, no Tannoy, no adrenaline-fuelled screams, no noisy chatter from the queue. It was almost preternaturally quiet, as if she were in some alternate dimension; in the theme park and yet not of it.

It was as if the ride wasn't running at all…

The blood rushed to her head, pounding loudly in her ears as she looked up at the twisting circular rails, so very thin, so very high. But with hideous clarity Clara already knew what she would see. A train lying like a broken toy along the curve of a loop, completely still, the passengers suspended high above the ground below, immobile.

It doesn't mean she's up there.

But there was no queue; the waiting people were being cleared away from the area by efficient staff members. No jaunty blazers and hats here; they were all purpose with fluorescent jackets and walkie-talkies and grim, unsmiling faces.

Clara turned and walked back to the café. They were meeting her there; she should have waited. Summer would be disappointed at having missed her turn and Raff would just be relieved that they hadn't been on that particular carriage and she would admit that for one terrified moment she had thought they were up there and Summer would roll her eyes and tell her to stop worrying about everything and they would agree to call it a day and walk back to the van…

Clara caught her breath. It was all going to be fine.

She walked back into the café, ready to catch her daughter up in her arms and never let her go.

They weren't there. She looked around, her head buzzing with disbelief. They had to be here.

'Are you all right?' The young man behind the counter was looking at her oddly as if he had never seen a woman utterly paralysed by fear, burdened by coats and indecision and terror before.

'Yes,' she said automatically, barely recognising the high, strained voice coming out of her mouth. 'At least, I don't know what to do. I think my daughter is on that train but I don't know who to ask.'

The room was spinning recklessly round, a rushing sound in her ears, and she swayed as if she were on a roller coaster herself, the coats spilling from her arms. Strong arms caught her, sat her down; voices were jabbering at her, asking questions she had no idea how to answer.

She had taken her eye well and truly off the ball and now her daughter was trapped alone except for a man she didn't know at all. And it was all Clara's fault.

CHAPTER TEN

'WHAT'S HAPPENING?'

That was a very good question. Unfortunately Raff wasn't sure he knew the answer. Carefully, making sure he didn't rock the carriage in any way, he turned his head to the side so that he could see Summer. She was holding herself still, her body was unnaturally rigid and the pointed little face was pale but she didn't seem to be on the verge of tears, thank goodness, Raff had never had to deal with weeping children before; doing so trapped two hundred metres in the air would definitely be beyond him.

'I think there's been a problem with the power,' he said as calmly as he could, trying not to dwell on just how uncomfortable it was to be suspended on his back strapped into a leather harness.

Although he believed there were clubs that catered for such desires.

At least the carriage hadn't stopped when they were facing down; there might have been mass hysteria. Instead he could look up at the late afternoon sky and pretend the ground was just a few comfortable feet below.

'Will they rescue us?' Her voice sounded small and scared.

'Of course!' Although goodness knew when. It was

hard to see exactly where they were and what was nearby but the ride extended out well over a kilometre and the entrance platform was a long way back. 'They won't want us cluttering up the park much longer.'

'How?'

'I think they'll use a crane,' he said after some thought. 'Although a helicopter would be fun. Have you ever been in one?'

'No.' Summer sounded wistful. 'Nor an aeroplane. Not even the Eurotunnel. We usually go away with Granny and Grandpa and stay in a cottage and walk.' She sounded less than thrilled.

'That sounds fun,' he said gravely.

'I want to stay in a villa with a pool like Natasha. Mummy says one day when our ship comes in. Although I'd rather fly there.'

Raff wanted to promise her that he'd take her away immediately, anywhere she wanted to go, but he managed to stop the words slipping out. He had no right to promise this child anything.

'Where would you want to go? If you could go anywhere?'

'Well,' she said thoughtfully. 'Natasha always goes to Majorca and that does look epic but I really want to go to Florida and go on all the roller coasters.'

She wanted to what? Raff didn't think he was ever going to set foot on a roller coaster again. 'They have alligators in Florida,' he said.

'Awesome! Have you seen one?'

'Yep, and crocodiles too. Big nasty ones in Africa.'

'You've been to Africa?' Her eyes were big with excitement. 'Did you see elephants and lions and zebras?'

'All of them. There's nothing like lying in a tent and listening to a lion roar somewhere in the distance.' He lowered his voice. 'It makes the hairs on the back of your neck stand up.'

'Ooh.' She sounded envious. 'Have you been to Australia?'

'Actually, no.'

'I was born there,' she said proudly.

'So you've been somewhere I haven't been.'

There was another long pause. 'Raff?'

'Mmm?'

'I'm scared.'

'Look at me.' Raff wiped all tension off his face and smiled reassuringly at her. 'Give me your hand.' Her hand was so small it looked lost in his; he clasped it tightly, giving her a reassuring squeeze. 'I promise you, Summer, we'll be absolutely fine. I am going to be with you the whole time, okay?'

'Okay.'

'Now, where else do you want to go? I've never seen the Northern Lights so that's on my list.' He felt the small hand relax and saw a little colour come back into her cheeks. She was going to be fine; he just hoped that rescue wasn't too far away.

If this was just a tiny proportion of the weight of responsibility Clara carried then no wonder she didn't want her daughter to go anywhere or do anything. If he ever became a parent then he would build a house lined with cotton wool and keep his children confined within. How did anybody do it? Carry that burden? No wonder his mother had run the second she had been left solely responsible for Polly and him.

For the first time Raff felt a glimmering of empathy for his sweet, childlike but ultimately weak mother. Pampered, cossetted her whole life, she had been utterly unprepared for life as a single mother. So she had run away; as he had, as Polly had. It must be in the genes.

But they had been so young, even younger than Summer here, and they had put all their faith and trust in her. She had let them down, badly. He couldn't imagine anything that would induce Clara to abandon Summer—or anything that would induce him to abandon his children if he was ever lucky enough to have any.

Children had never been in his life plan. But lying here, looking up at the stars, cradling a small trusting hand and listening to Summer describe her perfect holiday villa, they suddenly didn't seem like such a terrible idea after all.

'Miss.' One voice seemed more insistent than the rest and Clara forced herself to look up, to try and focus. 'Drink this.'

Tea. Hot, milky and full of sugar, utterly disgusting, but she managed a few sips and the room came back into focus. Clara pushed the still-full mug away but the man pushed it back. 'Drink it up, all of it,' he said and, like a child, she obeyed.

He didn't say another word, not until the mug was half empty. 'Your daughter is on Typhoon?'

'I think so.' She sounded more like herself. 'But I wasn't there. I don't know if she got on that train but she was supposed to meet me here.' Clara looked around. There were a few people staring at her curiously, some more openly than others; she focused on a couple of white-faced groups, possibly also worrying about trapped friends and relatives. 'She's only ten.'

'My name is Steve and I'm a customer service manager here. If you feel up to walking then you could accompany me to the site. The camera automatically photos them as the carriage goes horizontal, for souvenir photos, you know? If your daughter is on there then you'll be able to identify her.'

'Where else could she be?'

'We evacuated the area so she may just be waiting for you at the other side,' Steve said calmly. 'Is she on her own?'

Clara shook her head. 'No, she's with my friend, but his phone is here. I was watching their stuff…' Her voice faltered. Watching their coats, phones, but not them.

She should have been there.

'Okay, then, if you're able to walk, let's go.' Clara nodded numbly. But she didn't need to identify any photos. She knew that Summer was stuck on top of the narrow metal loop in the sky.

The next half-hour was the longest of Clara's life. She managed to phone her parents, relieved when they promised to be there as soon as possible. At least Summer wasn't on her own. Raff would be great in a crisis like this; calm, probably finding ways to make the whole thing a big adventure.

He'd keep her daughter safe.

The waiting friends and families had all been asked to wait in the café where tea, coffee and biscuits were on constant supply.

'They have come to a stop in the worst possible place,' Steve explained to the assembled group as they settled in. A few were in tears, a couple more red-faced and angry, demanding they be listened to and threatening lawsuits, but most, like Clara, seemed dazed. 'It's one of the highest points of the ride and there's no infrastructure nearby we can reach them from. Nor can we safely restart the ride. But we do plan for these worst-case scenarios and help is on the way. We've ascertained that no one is injured…' a relieved murmur broke out at his words '…and although they're not comfortable they're steady and despite appearances they are safe. Specialist rescue workers are bringing in cranes and ropes and we hope to begin freeing them within the hour.'

Clara sank into a chair, her hands cradling one in an endless loop of hot teas people kept putting in front of her. She didn't drink any of them, just held them, letting the warmth travel through her numbness, keeping her anchored in the present, keeping away her fears until she finally heard the news the group had been praying for: the first passenger had been safely brought back down to the ground. The rescue mission was working.

'Mummy!'

At last, at last. Clara was on her feet, pulling Summer close as if she could absorb her daughter back into her, inhaling her in. 'Hi, Sunshine.' Her voice was shaky and she tried to control it. 'I don't think I've ever been happier to see you.'

She stood back a little, anxiously checking her daughter over. There were no signs of strain or tears on Summer's face. In fact, she looked as if she had just strolled over from the carousel next ride over.

'Did you know Raff has been in a helicopter and one of those tiny planes?' Summer tucked herself back under Clara's arm, encircling her waist with her arms and squeezing in tight. 'He's heard lions at night and hyenas. Isn't that the coolest?'

'Totally. Are you okay, Sum? Was it scary?'

'A little,' her daughter confessed. 'But Raff made it all okay. He promised we'd be all right and we were. Wait till they hear about this at school. Natasha is going to be epically jealous.'

'Is she all right?'

Clara's heart missed a beat at the low, concerned voice.

'They took her off first. I just wanted to make sure she was okay.'

'Raff!' Summer left her mother's side and threw herself at the tall, broad man. He stood, awkward for a moment, before wrapping his arms around her and cuddling her back.

A lump formed in Clara's throat, making it hard to speak. This was what Summer should have had, had never had.

'If I ever get stuck on a roller coaster again I want to be stuck with you,' Raff told her daughter seriously. 'You were by far the best-behaved person up there.'

'Some of them were making the most awful racket,' Summer said, hanging onto Raff's arm. 'As if crying was going to make it better.'

'That's why I'm so glad you were there to cheer me up.'

Summer turned to Clara, her face lit up with excitement. 'Can we still go to dinner, Mummy, please? I'm totally okay.'

Clara swallowed. 'Sorry, honey.' There, that was normal, wasn't it? Not a quiver in her voice. 'Granny and Grandpa are just through there waiting to take you home. But I think they mentioned something about fish and chips...'

'I wanted to stay with you and Raff.'

'I'm just going to drive Raff home and then I'll be straight there. Come on, sweetie.'

She hadn't looked at him. Not properly. Raff just stood there as Summer was peeled off him and delivered to her grandparents, still protesting that she was okay and wanted to go out for dinner.

He wanted to placate her, promise her that it would happen some other time. But he wasn't sure about that at all.

'I'm sorry about that.' Clara still wasn't looking at him directly. 'I thought she'd be better off going straight back.'

'I could have driven the van back, if you wanted to go with Summer.'

She paused. 'I wasn't sure if you'd be okay to drive. Besides, I thought we should talk.'

Here it came. Raff was suddenly very tired. There had been a few moments up there when he had been concerned, worried that they'd be trapped for several hours, that the actual rescue process would be dangerous. The responsibility had been heavy.

It was funny; he bore a huge amount of responsibility nearly every day of his life. He had to keep all kinds of facilities going; literally hundreds of lives depended on him. He took that responsibility very seriously, lived for it. But it was nothing compared to the fear he had felt when Clara's daughter was in such terrible danger and there was nothing he could do but sit there, talk to her and hold her hand.

He ran a hand through his hair, aware just how much the accident had taken out of him. All he wanted to do at this point was have a beer, a shower and collapse into his bed, but there was no point putting this off.

Clara would say what she had to say; she had every right to. He had messed up.

They walked away from the building, their steps in harmony but several inches apart, not one centimetre of them touching.

'I'm sorry,' he said after a while, not able to bear the silence any longer. 'You must have been terrified.'

Clara stopped and stood stock still for a long, long moment. Raff could see how unnaturally rigid her shoulders were, the lack of colour in her lips. The defeated look in her eyes.

'You had no right.' Her voice was trembling; he didn't know if she was holding back tears or filled with anger. He feared it was both.

Her throat was burning with the effort of keeping the tears held back. Again. For goodness' sake, she had barely cried in years and now she was giving Niobe a run for her watery money.

'You had no right,' she tried again. 'Inviting us here in front of Summer so I had no choice but to agree, offering to accompany her on the ride. I know I could have said no.' She could hear the volume of her voice rising and took a deep breath. 'I could have but you put me in a really difficult position. I've hardly been around lately, thanks to you. The last thing I wanted to be was a killjoy mother as well as an absent one!'

She expected him to defend himself, to get angry back. Instead he stood, facing her, palms outstretched. 'You're right. I was completely out of line.'

If he thought being calm and reasonable was going to calm her down he was in for a big shock. 'She could have been killed up there!' The words were torn out of her, raw and heartfelt. 'Do you know how it feels to see the one person, the one person you would gladly die for, stuck miles up in the sky and know you are utterly, utterly helpless? Of course you don't!' Was that her? So cold and bitter. 'The only person you care for is yourself.'

Raff's face whitened. 'I care about you.'

She didn't want to hear it. 'Yes, one day at a time.' Was that why she was so angry? They hadn't finished the conversation in her office; Summer had interrupted them before it had been resolved. No, she pushed the uncomfortable thought far out of her mind. It had nothing to do with Raff and his piecemeal approach to relationships; this was all about her daughter.

'She could have died,' she repeated and this time the words really hit home. 'She could have fallen and I wasn't there, Raff. I wasn't there.'

'No, you weren't, but I was.' He ran a hand down her arm, looking intently into her eyes and just like that the anger dissipated. Oh, how she wanted to step forward, lean into him and let him hold her. But she stood firm. 'She wasn't alone. And, Clara? Your daughter was amazing. She's brave and interesting and that is down to you. You are a wonderful mother.'

He was saying all the right things and it would be so, so easy to put this behind her, behind them, and let him into her life properly, into Summer's life. Because this was what Summer wanted, what she deserved. Someone who appreciated just how special she was, someone who made her feel safe.

This was what Clara needed.

But Raff wasn't that man as much as she desperately wanted him to be. He was leaving, soon. And both she and Summer deserved better than a part-time Prince Charming.

'Come on.' She resumed walking, relieved to see the van close by. 'I'll drive you home.'

Raff didn't even try and argue, just slid across to the passenger seat as Clara opened the door and settled herself at the wheel. Neither of them spoke during the short drive back to Hopeford. It was no time at all until Clara drew up in front of the pretty cottage and killed the engine—and Raff still had no idea what to say, how to break the deathly silence.

He had always been able to rely on his charm in the past. Now it wasn't enough, not by miles.

'I know people think I keep her too close.' The words made him jump, unexpected in the long silence. 'But they have no idea what she and I have been through. When I first came back I was so young, other mothers used to think I was her au pair or big sister. I always had to do everything better to prove I was as good as they were.'

'Of course you were.' He could see her. Young, independent, tilting her head coolly as she walked past the whispers, the sneers, the judgement. 'Better.'

'I have to put her first,' she said. 'Always.'

'Clara.' He reached over and took her cold hand. 'I know today was horrible. I can't imagine what you went through. But it doesn't have to change anything.'

She was immobile under his touch, the green cat's eyes remote, shuttered. 'You're leaving,' she said. 'There isn't a future for us, so what's the point?'

Fun? Living for today? Attraction? Raff searched through his usual stock of reasons and arguments and found them wanting.

'I think we could be good together.'

'When you're in town, when you can fit us in? I know how amazing your job is, Raff. I think it's great, that you are a very giving person. I really do. But I can't be second best. And nor can Summer. And I don't think you can give us what we need.'

Ouch. Words like arrows, well aimed and sharp. Raff looked at her and could see no indecision; her eyes were steady, the colour of a stormy sea. 'She deserves better than that, Raff. *I* deserve better. She needs a father figure, someone she can rely on. I know you were great with her up there and I am so grateful but I can't have you in her life. I can't have you in my life.'

Raff wanted to reassure her but what could he say? He couldn't offer her more, couldn't *be* more. His life was elsewhere; his calling was elsewhere. She was right. She deserved so much more than an emotionally stilted runaway could offer her.

'You do,' he said, aware how harsh his voice sounded. He swallowed, shocked at the size of the lump in his throat. 'You both do. I hope you find someone who appreciates just how amazing you are.'

'You didn't promise me anything,' she said, looking down at her hands, twisting the bangle round and round her slender wrist. 'You were always very clear what this was and I thought I knew what I was doing. I guess somewhere along the way the lines blurred for me. That was stupid of me.' She looked up at him, held his gaze. 'But things are clear now. You're a good man, Raff Rafferty. I hope you find whatever it is you're looking for.'

She reached across and opened his door. Her intention was clear. Raff searched for something to say but came up with nothing. All he could do was press a kiss to her soft cheek and climb out of the van and watch as she drove away into the deepening twilight, leaving Raff alone with only the birds' evensong for company.

He was free just the way he liked it. Free of family obligations, free of Rafferty's, free of all ties. It was what he had always wanted.

It should feel so good. So why did he feel as if he had suddenly lost everything?

CHAPTER ELEVEN

'WHAT YOU NEED to do,' Maddie said, 'is get back on the horse.'

'I need to *what*?' Clara stared at her cousin suspiciously.

'Get back on the horse. So you fell. Who can blame you? That man was sex on a stick. I would have quite liked to have fallen myself, if I wasn't with Ollie,' Maddie finished, a little unconvincingly, Clara thought. 'And as a starter to get you back into the swing of things he was perfect. But he was never the main course and you know it, so don't let him make you lose your appetite.' She sat back on the sofa, took a sip of her wine and beamed at Clara.

Clara tried to disentangle Maddie's mix of metaphors and gave up. 'I still don't know what to do about this.' She held up the cheque that had arrived with that morning's post. 'It's twice the amount I was expecting.'

'Which is terrible because?'

Clara gave her a level look. 'Because I was sleeping with him.'

'It's guilt money. He knows he should have stayed and fought for you. He hasn't and he's throwing money at his guilty conscience.'

'I didn't want him to stay and fight for me. I'm not Guinevere.' But Clara could feel her cheeks heating up;

even she didn't believe a single word she was saying. She knew with utter certainty that they would echo through her head tonight as she fought off thoughts of him. It was worse at night, what-ifs and might-have-beens spiralling dizzily through her mind until she finally fell into a fitful, dream-filled sleep. 'I don't know if I can accept this. Should I return it, ask for the right amount?'

'Don't you dare.' Maddie sat bolt upright in horror. 'You deserve that money. And as you are giving away that whole gorgeous wardrobe he bought you…'

'*Gave* me and I'm not giving it away, I'm selling it. All proceeds to Doctors Everywhere.' She was never going to wear most of them again; this seemed like the right solution.

'Every item?' Maddie peeped over from under long eyelashes but Clara had seen her cousin perform that trick far too many times before to fall for her beseeching glance.

'Every one.'

'Even the sequinned shift?'

'Even the sequinned shift, well, probably.' She hated to admit it but she did have a secret fondness for the frivolous, shiny, ridiculously short piece of clothing. Nothing to do with the look in Raff's eyes when she had first tried it on.

'Bags me it next time we go out!' Maddie was all smiles again. 'Seriously, Clara, that's one hell of a bonus for a job well done. Whatever his motivation you put in a lot of hours—legitimate hours—and he got the results he wanted. Take the cheque and get yourself signed up to one of these websites before you retreat back into that shell of yours.' She patted the open laptop perched between them. 'Right, what are your interests? Fine dining and culture?'

'No!' Clara shook her head, uneasily aware that she was being a little over-emphatic. 'I did far too much of that with Raff.'

'And you didn't enjoy it?'

An image came into Clara's head. Mud. Mud everywhere, Raff hoisting her up onto the rope. The feeling of freedom, of being able to let go. 'I want someone I can do ordinary things with,' she said slowly. 'Walk, talk, read. But when we do them together they become extraordinary.'

There was a long moment's silence. 'Don't we all?' said Maddie softly.

Clara picked up the cheque again, aware she had said too much, revealed too much even to herself. 'I'm not going to sign up yet, no...' as her cousin tried to interrupt '...I don't mean I won't, just not tonight. Not right now. I think I might take Summer away for a few weeks and I'll do it when we get back.'

'But it's term time. You never let her miss school.'

'I think this is a sign.' Clara looked at the cheque. She had already been considering the trip before the cheque arrived. It just made the logistics easier. 'I'll put the amount I was expecting into the business, just as I always planned to. But the extra I'm going to spend doing something I should have done a long time ago. I'm going to take Summer to Australia.'

Australia. Once it had been the promised land—a land of freedom, of exotic, alien landscapes, of opportunity. And then it had all turned to gritty dust. For the longest time she couldn't even hear an Australian accent without a sense of foreboding, of panic. Had put her wanderlust behind her, packed her need for adventure away along with her backpack and guidebooks and dreams.

But in doing so she had denied Summer her heritage. Her daughter deserved to know who she was. And Clara? Clara needed to find herself again. 'I think I was attracted to Raff because he reminded me of how I used to be.'

Maddie snorted. 'You were attracted to him because he was hot.'

Clara smiled. But the painful thump her heart gave whenever she thought of him, the tightness in her chest, had nothing to do with the way he looked, nice as that was. It was the way he made her feel—as if she could do anything. Once she had had that belief in herself.

'That too,' she agreed. 'But if this whole mess has taught me anything it's that I need to figure some things out about me before I can commit to anyone properly. It's a good thing Raff was always going away.' See, that was convincing. She was totally believable. 'I'm not ready for a relationship. Not yet. But I hope to be.' She smiled brightly. An easy, simple relationship. They existed, right?

'And Byron?'

'I hope he'll meet up with us but if he doesn't?' She shrugged. 'I can't force him, Maddie. I used to think if he just met Summer he'd fall for her but now I just don't know. But she should see where she was born, where she spent her first year.'

It was time to lay some ghosts to rest. And when she came back she'd be ready to move on, Raff Rafferty nothing but a pleasant memory. See, she had a plan. Everything was better with a plan. Even a bruised heart.

And that was all this was. She'd allowed herself to believe their own story, that was all. Hearts didn't get broken, not in real life, not after just a few weeks, not when you were the one to walk away, the one with responsibilities.

No, it was just a little bruised. She just needed time,.

Time, distance and a little bit of hope that it was all going to be all right, somehow.

But later, when Maddie had gone and Clara was sitting alone on her sofa, as she always was, that tiny bit of hope evaporated.

She was a strong woman, she owned her own business, her own home, raised her daughter alone. Was it wrong for her to have wanted him to ride into battle for her? Wanted him to try?

She was no fairy-tale princess but right now she would give anything to see Raff on a charger fighting his way through a forest of thorns, scaling a tower, searching the town for the owner of one small slipper. Instead he had turned and walked away without a word.

As Byron had.

Was she that unlovable? Wasn't she worth fighting for? He hadn't said one word to try and convince her to change her mind.

Clara looked around the small room. At the large framed prints and photos she had carefully chosen and hung, the wallpaper she had spent days cutting, pasting and hanging and smoothing out most of the air bubbles.

The sofa she and Summer hung out on, chatted, watched films, read books, cuddled on. The plants she tried not to kill with alternate bouts of love and neglect. The stuffed bookshelves, an eclectic mix of Summer's old picture books, the ones that were too babyish to stay in her room but that Clara couldn't bear to part with, crime novels and business guides. No travel guides though. Maybe it was time to get them out again.

This was her life, the life she chose and worked every minute to maintain. A safe, ordered life. And now it wasn't enough.

She missed him, a huge aching chasm inside her that

hurt more with every day, every non phone call, every non email. She didn't want any of the perfect matches on the dating sites; she wanted Raff.

But he didn't want her.

It was as if the sun had gone out and she didn't know if she was ever going to get used to living in the dull grey gloom. She had to get away. She would take Summer to Australia and while she was there she would forget all about Raff Rafferty.

It was the only way.

'Castor.' His grandfather stood to meet him, every inch the proprietor. He might have been forced into retirement but here, in the world-famous Rafferty tea rooms, he was still king. 'Good to see you.'

'And you, sir.' Raff took the proffered hand and shook it. 'Good to see you out and about.'

'Got no time to play the damned invalid,' his grandfather grunted as he slowly sat down. Raff watched him anxiously but it didn't seem more than the usual twinges of arthritis that had plagued Charles Rafferty for the last few years. He turned to the discreetly hovering waitress. 'We'll have the usual, Birgitte.'

'Should you be eating afternoon tea? Wouldn't the soup be a better option?'

Charles Rafferty scowled. 'I've been eating pap for the last few weeks. A man can't live on soup alone.'

'Nor can he live long on huge amounts of cream and butter, especially after suffering problems with his heart,' Raff reminded him. He turned to the waitress and smiled. 'Can you make sure there is no cream or butter and just a small selection of cakes? Thank you so much.'

'You always did think you knew best.' But to Raff's relief his grandfather made no attempt to countermand his order. Instead he sat back in his chair and turned his trademark sharp look on Raff. The one that had him confessing all his sins instantly. 'Polly returns soon and all this...' he waved one hand at the tearooms '...all this will be hers. Any regrets?'

'Only that it took this long,' he assured him.

'And you? Where next?'

Now *that* was the million-dollar question. Raff's morning meeting at Doctors Everywhere had changed everything and Raff had no idea how he felt about any of it. He waited until the waitress had unloaded the heavy tray, positioning the silver teapot in the middle of the table, accompanied by a silver jug of hot water, a jug of milk, a small bowl of lemon slices and the silver sugar bowl. It was the same design and arrangement as the very first afternoon tea served in this very room nearly one hundred years ago. Rafferty's were big on tradition.

'Jordan,' he said, pouring out his grandfather's tea, knowing he liked it weak, black and with lemon. He wasn't so fussy; in the camps he took his hot drinks as they were served, grateful for the comfort and the caffeine. 'Just for a few weeks.' He stirred his own tea, finding it hard to look him in the eye, not wanting his response to influence him in any way.

'But they want me to consider basing myself back here. Their Director of Philanthropy is moving on and they've asked me to replace him.'

He continued to stir his tea, the morning's conversation still whirling around his brain.

He had gone to the London office to report for duty and organise his next posting, a normal procedure that had quickly proven to be far from standard when he had been ushered, not to the assignments department but into the CEO's office for a long and frank conversation.

'You're one of our best guys out in the field,' the CEO had said. 'But you're replaceable out there. I'd like you to consider working here instead. We completely beat our targets at that ball, and signed up some committed new sponsors; much of that was through your contacts. With you heading up our philanthropy section, combining your business experience with the work you did with us, I reckon we could bring in some serious money—and that means funding some serious work.'

'Obviously you would be good in that role. I trained you myself.' His grandfather was being as modest as usual. 'But you always hated being deskbound. I thought it was the field work you wanted?'

Raff had to fight the urge to squirm. With his grandfather's keen gaze focused on him like this there was no way he could lie to him—or to himself.

'Honestly? I'd been thinking something along similar lines myself,' he admitted. 'It makes a lot of sense, I know. But it will be hard. I love the unpredictability of what I do now. They've promised it won't all be desk work and meetings and events. I'll need to have a good understanding of our needs so I'll still get to spend some time in the field, but it will be site visits from the HQ, not getting my hands dirty and being part of a team, at least not in the same way. But everyone at HQ needs to do at least one field rotation every two years so I wouldn't have to walk away entirely.'

'Is this about the girl? Your grandmother thinks she's the one.'

'When did you see Grandmother?' Raff didn't want to talk about Clara, not to someone who could read him as well as his grandfather did.

'We *are* still married,' his grandfather pointed out as if separate lives and separate houses for the last ten years were a mere technicality. 'But we're not discussing my love life.' Raff choked on his tea. Thank goodness, now *that* would be an awkward conversation in every way. Grandparents weren't supposed to have love lives, especially not ones who were estranged. Bridge partners? Absolutely. Love lives? Absolutely not. 'Wouldn't this new job work much better if you are considering getting engaged?'

'We're not.' With relief Raff turned to the waitress bearing the heavy stand heaped with dainty finger sandwiches, scones and an array of tiny cakes and pastries. 'Thanks so much, Birgitte. Grandfather, don't get up. I'll serve you.'

'Only to make sure I eat brown bread and no cake,' his grandfather grumbled. He looked keenly at Raff. 'I thought things were serious? You've been inseparable for weeks. I admit I wasn't sure at first but actually I quite like her. She's feisty, good thing for a spoilt chap like you.'

Raff took longer selecting each sandwich than was strictly necessary, placing them carefully on the plate. 'It hasn't worked out,' he said, handing him the plate with the elegant flourish a summer working in this very tea room had instilled in him.

'Why ever not? You were smitten.' Charles Rafferty pointed his fork at Raff in a way that would have got either he or Polly sent from the table when they were children.

Smitten. Clara had obviously fooled everyone even better than he had hoped. It helped that he liked her, that he desired her, that he enjoyed getting behind the barriers she put up, making her laugh. He valued her opinion, enjoyed her company—and sometimes the sight of her almost brought him to his knees.

But *smitten*?

'Clara deserves more than I can give her. She needs someone reliable, someone who won't run away the moment things get difficult.' He had told himself this so many times in the last week it sounded as if he were reciting something he had learned off by heart.

'And why is that someone not you?'

Raff opened his mouth to reply and then shut it again, more than a little nonplussed. His grandfather was sitting bolt upright looking expectantly at him, wanting some sort of answer. How could he not know? He was separated from his own wife after all! The Raffertys were all the same: good workers, terrible husbands. Or wives—Polly was no nearer to being settled than he was. They'd probably end up living together in their nineties in a crumbling mansion somewhere and people would call them 'those peculiar Rafferty twins'.

They were impetuous—he had signed up to a crisis organisation on a whim, for goodness' sake—the absolute opposite of the calm, ordered, organised Clara. Raff curled his fingers into his palm. He had to stop thinking about her. She needed a future with someone stable. Someone unlike him.

The honourable, the only thing to do was to respect her wishes, to walk away.

'You did spend six years working in a business you dislike for my sake.'

'I wouldn't say dislike…'

'Four years working for little money in difficult conditions helping others?'

'Well, I…'

'You came home the second your sister needed you?'

'Of course, but…'

His keen blue eyes softened. 'You wrote to your

mother every week even though she never wrote back. Visited your father every weekend even though he had no idea who you were. Rejected invitations to parties, the chance to be in the school team because they clashed with visiting hours.'

How did his grandfather know all this? Know *him* this well? Raff thought he'd done such a good job of keeping it all hidden well away. 'They were my parents.' He coughed slightly to clear his throat, dislodge the unwanted lump that was suddenly lodged there. He hadn't wanted to turn down those invitations, to lose his coveted spot in the team, but what if that had been the week? What if his father had died and he hadn't visited, hadn't told him once again how sorry he was for not saving him?

His mother seldom replied to the letters he dutifully sent. Occasionally parcels would turn up, books or T-shirts or toys. After a couple of years they had become even less frequent—and the toys were too young, the books too easy, the clothes a size or so too small.

'Of course she wants you,' his grandfather said, taking advantage of Raff's introspection to help himself to several of the cakes. 'You're a good man, Castor, loyal to a fault, hardworking, handsome. Well…' his eyes twinkled '…people do say you take after me. The only person who doesn't believe in you, Castor, is you.'

He put his knife down and looked seriously over the table at Raff. 'Don't make the same mistakes I did. Don't walk away because you're too stubborn or too proud or too afraid. You don't want to be my age and full of regrets. They make lonely bedfellows, you know. If I'd tried harder with your grandmother, then maybe…' He sighed. 'I have hope it's not too late for us. You at your age? You should be beating her door down, begging her to take you back.'

Raff saw his grandfather out to his car, his mind whirling. The job, Clara, his grandfather. Clara again. What if he let her down? Couldn't be the man she needed him to be?

There was more than his pride at stake here. More than his heart. He was willing to risk all he was, all he wanted, all his dreams, gamble them on a chance of happiness. But could he risk Clara's, Summer's stability? Their future?

It was so much responsibility. The stakes were far, far too high. Better to fold now than let them lose everything. That was the right thing to do no matter how very wrong it felt.

But try as he might to convince himself a small beacon of hope refused to flicker and die away. What if it wasn't too late? What if he could somehow make things right?

What if this was the chance he'd been waiting for his whole life? Was he just going to sit back and let the opportunity to be part of a family pass him by? He had salvaged his relationship with his grandfather despite all the odds. Maybe, just maybe there was hope for him after all.

CHAPTER TWELVE

IT SHOULD HAVE BEEN utter bliss, lying on a comfortable chaise, the sun blissfully melting into every one of her weary bones and muscles. She didn't even have Summer to worry about; she was currently enjoying a playdate with an old friend of Clara's, an afternoon of beaches, barbecues and rollerblades. She wouldn't be missing Clara at all.

But no matter how comfortable the chaise, how delicious the sun, how novel the lack of responsibility, Clara just couldn't relax. With an exasperated groan she sat up and checked her phone again, hoping someone, somewhere needed her. No, there were no texts, voicemails, emails or any other type of message.

She was utterly alone.

Looking around the lavish poolside area, Clara tried to shake off the gloom. After all, look where she was! Sitting in a comfortable chair, an iced juice on the table beside her, views to die for spread out all around her; blue, blue water overshadowed by the wings of the famous opera house.

She was living the dream, for a few days at least. She had decided to finish their holiday in luxurious style and you really didn't get much more luxurious than her present location.

If she didn't want her admittedly extortionately expensive drink, then she could go for a swim in the rooftop pool just a few feet in front of her, or work out in the lavishly appointed gym, have a nap in the massive hotel room that Summer swore was bigger than their entire apartment or go for a walk. She was just steps from the Rocks Markets and she still had some gifts to buy. If nothing in the touristy stalls tempted her then there were plenty of shops in Sydney's historic heart.

Or she could go to the Botanic Gardens; after all, she told herself, she'd just be taking a walk. She wouldn't be stressing about tomorrow. About the near miracle that was going to occur.

No. Clara slumped back in her chair with a sigh, her eyes unfocused, barely noticing the spectacular scenery. All she could see was the exotic lush greenery of the gardens and the two people who would be strolling there tomorrow. Would they have anything to say to each other? What would be worse: awkward silences or an instant connection?

This was what you wanted, she told herself, as if repeating the words over and over again would somehow make them true. Summer was finally going to meet her father. Clara just hadn't expected to feel so terrified about it.

If she was honest with herself then she might have to admit it wasn't just today, this loneliness. It had been chilling her for weeks even as she had busied herself with preparations for this trip. They had spent the first ten days here in Sydney staying with old friends before heading out to the Blue Mountains, taking in the vineyard where they had lived when Summer was just a baby.

After that they had undertaken the long, exhausting

journey to the farm where one of Clara's friends had moved to, completely in the middle of nowhere. Her daughter had immediately taken to the outdoor life; loving every minute of her first riding lessons, hanging onto a strap as she was bounced around in the back of the truck, swimming in the local watering hole. *Don't,* Clara had wanted to cry out a hundred times. *Look out for crocodiles, for snakes, for spiders, what if the horse bolts or the truck overturns?*

What if?

But she had held her tongue even though it had physically hurt, even though she had been almost doubled up in fear and dread, and she had watched her daughter blossom.

Meanwhile Clara herself found it harder and harder to work out just who she was any more.

The trip had definitely healed some old wounds, but had also brought up new, troubling ones. Even after all the years away she had friends here, people who she could connect with straight away. There was no one outside her family who she had that connection with back in England. No one but Raff.

Damn, she had said his name. If it weren't bad enough torturing herself with images of Summer and Byron getting on so well she became totally redundant, she had to think of Raff. Again.

Truth be told he was often on her mind. The more she tried to forget about him, the larger he loomed.

Because as good a time as she was having, as much fun as it was showing Australia to her daughter, there was a little part of her that knew that having Raff with them would have made everything perfect. He'd have charmed her friends and adored the outback. And if he were here she would feel so much better about tomorrow, if he were distracting her, reassuring her that she was doing the right thing.

She was, wasn't she? Mechanically Clara reached for the bangle at her wrist, turning it round and round, the familiar feel of the silver slipping through her fingertips a reassurance, a grounding.

Typical Byron to leave his change of heart to the last minute, for the grand reconciliation to eat into their last days. But how could she deny him? Well, she would happily deny him anything and everything but this wasn't about him.

Unfortunately though it was about her, because, sitting here alone, she had to admit that once you took away her work and her daughter there was very little left.

She had allowed her worry for Summer, her drive to provide for her daughter, to consume her. Which was laudable. But, there that word was again, it was a little lonely.

Well, things would change. She would date and she would not compare every man to Raff, no matter how tempting. She would have hobbies and friends and relax and soon she wouldn't even remember Raff's name.

Or think about him whenever she looked at the night sky and saw the Heavenly Twins. Thank goodness they had different stars here in the Southern Hemisphere.

Clara eyed her phone again, her pulse speeding up. What harm would one little peek do? He hadn't blogged for a couple of weeks now; she just wanted to know he was all right. It wasn't stalking or being obsessive. It was caring about a friend.

It was almost embarrassing how quickly her browser picked up the Doctors Everywhere website, how it immediately assumed she wanted to go to the section dedicated to field staff blogs. It was almost as if she had been

reading it every day. Every evening. When she couldn't
sleep…

Not just Raff's blog, all of them. Trying to get an idea
of the world he occupied, the people he worked with, his
friends, the way he spent his days. The job that was so
all consuming he walked away from his family, his heritage, to be part of it.

That he walked away from her without a backwards
look.

Her breath caught as she saw the all-too-familiar
photo. It was a couple of years old, she reckoned, the
hair shorter, more preppy, his gaze wary. Her finger hovered and for one moment she fooled herself that she had
a choice before she touched the screen and watched the
blog load.

Nothing new. It was the same short entry she had read
far too many times detailing his impressions on arriving
at the refugee camp. The same matter-of-fact tone as he
described families crammed into tents, all their worldly
goods reduced to what they could carry, how they were
treating pregnant women who had walked for hundreds
of miles, malnourished children, broken men.

It was so vivid she could see it; every time the shock
hit her anew. His work was so important, how could she
compete? What if she asked him to come back and he re-
gretted it, that regret poisoning whatever it was they had?

Or maybe they had nothing and he wouldn't come
back at all.

Or what if she risked it? Let him go and welcomed
him home in between postings. Shared him with the job
he loved so much. Could she do that? Could she be so
selfless, live with the uncertainty and the danger and the
long months when he was away?

She turned the bangle round and round. That question had become more and more pressing as the weeks went by. She wanted to answer yes...

'Excuse me, miss?' The polite young waiter had returned, a tall glass on his tray.

'I haven't finished this one yet,' she apologised with a guilty look at the still-full drink. It was her third. She dreaded seeing how much money she had wasted on the freshly squeezed juices. But ordering them, sitting here with a drink and watching the world go by was better than sitting in her room and brooding. Just.

'No, miss, this is a new drink. It's a mudslide.'

'A what?' Clara stared at the drink. It looked like a coffee to her.

'A mudslide,' he repeated. 'Vodka, coffee liqueur and Irish cream, mixed with crushed ice.'

A latte with a kick. 'But I didn't order a drink. There must be some mistake.'

'No, miss, the gentleman over there ordered it. He said you were a big fan of mud.'

Clara stared at him. 'He said I...' Was this some strange Australian chat-up ritual? She had worked in a bar not that far from here throughout her pregnancy and for the first months of Summer's life but that was nearly a decade ago. Maybe this was a cultural reference that was totally lost on her.

The only mud she had been near in years was with Raff. Oh!

Don't be ridiculous, Clara told herself. Raff was in Jordan, but her heart was hammering so loud she was surprised the whole pool area wasn't throbbing with the beat. She swallowed, her mouth dry.

'The gentleman?' She could barely get the words out, torn between embarrassment and a longing so deep, so intense it nearly floored her.

'Over at the bar.' The young man nodded over towards the long pool bar the other side of the terrace.

It wasn't him; it couldn't be him. She was setting herself up for a massive disappointment but all the admonishing thoughts in the world couldn't quell the hope rising helium light inside her.

Clara tugged at her skirt as she rose out of the chair, looking over in the direction the waiter had indicated. *Be cool and say no, thank you,* the sensible side of her was whispering. *It'll be some bored businessman seeing you sitting alone. He thinks he'll liven his business trip up with a flirt. That's all it is.*

And just because he has broad shoulders and a shock of dishevelled dirty blond hair and navy blue eyes, even darker with exhaustion, doesn't mean it's him. It can't be him sauntering slowly towards you.

'I thought it was apt.' He nodded at the drink still sitting on the waiter's tray. Raff lifted it off, discreetly passing the young man a folded note as he slunk gratefully back to the bar. 'In lieu of the real thing.'

Clara stood and stared, drinking him in. It was like the first time she had seen him: an old crumpled shirt, battered jeans, skin almost grey with weariness. Totally irresistible.

'I thought you were in Jordan.' Of all the things to say. But conversation had deserted her; she was stuck to the spot like an incredulous statue, unable to move or feel.

'I was two days ago, or was it three? It may have been a week. It feels like I've been travelling for ever.'

'But what are you doing here?' It was a mirage, surely. She was like a traveller in a desert, Raff the welcome oasis. Which made her a truly pathetic human being but all she wanted to do was look at him, relearn every feature for posterity. Instead she stood, a foot between them, too scared to touch him in case he disappeared.

'I wanted to see you.' Clara gaped at him, a mute question in her eyes. 'Maddie told me where you were. Nice surroundings, by the way. Is this how you backpacked as a teenager?'

'Just like this, five star all the way.' She fastened on his words. 'You came to see me?'

'I'm hoping to see a baby koala as well, it seems a shame to come all this way and not see one, but mainly I've come to see you.'

Heat filled her, whooshing up from her toes and filling every atom, every nerve burning. 'Me?'

'And the baby koala…' Raff gestured to the drink. 'Are you going to drink that?'

'Sorry.' It was such a lovely gesture and she was spoiling it. 'I'm not a huge fan of vodka. Or Irish cream.'

He regarded the brown mixture with distaste. 'It sounded better than it looks. Do you want to take a walk?'

'A walk?' For goodness' sake, it was as if she were under a spell. Raff was here. In the swanky terrace bar. Half the way across the world from where she had seen him last, from where he was supposed to be. She should have squealed, thrown herself at him, made some indication that she was pleased to see him instead of standing here gaping.

'I've not been to Sydney before. So far I have seen the airport, the inside of the taxi and this rather nice swimming pool. I have been reliably informed there is a rather impressive bridge and opera house I should take a look at. Where's Summer?'

'With a friend. Tomorrow she's seeing Byron.' It was

such a relief to tell him, the burden instantly slipping off her shoulders.

Raff raised his eyebrows in shock, letting out a low whistle of surprise.

'I know, I told him we were coming and made sure he knew when we would be in Sydney and heard nothing, which wasn't a surprise at all. Then he called last night. Which was a surprise but what could I say?' It was nice to see him, to hear him, to be able to speak to someone who absolutely, intuitively understood.

More than nice.

He grimaced. 'Anything you wanted but, knowing you, I guess you said that of course you could accommodate him at such short notice.'

Clara shrugged, the warmth in his eyes almost too much for comfort. 'For her sake.'

He nodded. 'I know. What time are you taking her?'

She bit her lip. 'He's going to text.'

'Do you want me to come with you?'

Just eight words. Eight simple words. Words that made all the fear and the loneliness and the worry evaporate in the hot Sydney sun.

'Yes, please.' She glanced at him, almost shyly. 'She'll be so happy to see you. She talks about you all the time.'

'I can't wait to see her either. I'm counting on her to teach me all the Aussie slang. And I bet she knows all the best baby koalas.'

'She knows it all.' Clara rolled her eyes.

The lift down was spacious and cool but to Clara it felt tiny, almost claustrophobic. She was sharing it with Raff. Every nerve tingled with the need, the want to touch him but she couldn't, frightened he'd disappear like a genie back into the bottle of her imagination. The lift opened straight into the impressive marble foyer and she mutely led the way to the exit. As they reached the steps the sun hit them bright and hot, as different from an English sun as a daisy from an orchid. Clara automatically began to walk on the harbourside path, the sea sparkling beneath them.

Raff took her hand, an easy, natural gesture. It felt like coming home. Clara allowed her fingers to curl up, to meet his, a lifeline she had thought she could manage without. 'So Cinderella is all alone in the big city? It's a good thing I've come to cheer you up.'

'You're the fairy godmother?'

He squeezed her fingers. 'Or Buttons, but I did have another role in mind.'

The teasing voice had turned serious as he stopped and turned to face her, still holding her hand in his. 'I walked away because it felt like the right thing to do. But it wasn't. It was the cowardly thing to do.' His fingers tightened, almost painfully but she didn't resist, his firm grip anchoring her down. 'I don't really know how families work, how loving someone works. It seems so easy to get it wrong, to let people down so badly it's worse than trying at all.'

Clara clung onto him, her fingers laced tightly through his, her heart hammering. 'I was afraid too,' she said honestly. 'I was losing my way. I spent so many years trying to keep things secure and safe and then you came along.' She shook her head, trying to blink away the tears threatening to fall. 'You made my life look so small. You made me feel small.'

'I didn't mean to.' He stepped forward in alarm, one hand brushing her cheek, collecting her tears as they overspilt. 'I just wanted to see you smile. God, it was presumptuous, I know, but I admit I liked the idea of shaking you up a little. You were so sorted, it made me feel inadequate.' He grimaced. 'That was wrong, sorry.'

'No, it was good,' she protested, holding his hand to her cheek. 'I needed it. If it wasn't for you I wouldn't be here, moving on. I'd just work and look after Summer and kid myself that I was happy with such a narrow life. But I'm not. And if loving you means long absences and worry and sharing you with your work then I can manage. Because that's a lot better than not having you in my life at all. And I do want you, I do love you.'

She'd said it. She'd said it all. The four-letter word she hadn't even admitted to herself on long, lonely, sleepless nights. The world might still be going on around them but here and now it had stopped as the word reverberated around her head.

Love.

She peeked up to see his reaction but Raff's face was unreadable.

'Would it ruin your plans too much if I was around a bit more than that?' he asked. 'If I was around pretty much full time? Thing is…' he grinned ruefully '…and I am being presumptuous again so please bear with me, the thing is I don't know much about being a good husband and father.' Clara's heart twisted at the words. 'But I am pretty sure being away over half the year is not a good start.'

'But you love your job.' It was a half-hearted statement, as her mind raced at his words. Had he really said husband and father?

'I love you more.' Raff trailed his hand along her cheek; every nerve fired up at the light caress. 'They offered me a job in London a few weeks ago and I said I needed time to think about it, but I was just scared. I defined myself through my job. I wasn't sure who I would be without it. But if I'm honest, I'd been thinking about offering my services full time in London anyway. The ball made me realise just how much I can achieve with my friends and connections—it would be pretty selfish of me not to use them. It's a very different kind of challenge but a good one, I think.

'Then when I was away all I could think about was you. Being out in the field wasn't enough any more. In fact...' his finger brushed her lip '...it was pretty lonely.'

'I've been lonely too.' It didn't feel like an admission of failure, not now.

'Suddenly, it didn't feel like such a big decision at all. I was going to take the job and woo you. Only when I hotfooted it to Hopeford you were gone.'

'So you came all the way to Sydney.' Clara smiled at him, a wide, uninhibited grin of joy. 'We leave in two days. You didn't have that long to wait.'

'What's another twenty-four hours of travel?' he said. 'Besides, waiting was making me anxious. I didn't want to lose my nerve. You can be pretty intimidating, you know, Clara Castleton?'

'Me?' She'd worked hard at it but that wasn't who she wanted to be any more. She was sick of keeping the world at arm's length.'

'You can also be funny and warm and sharp and there is no one I'd rather wade through mud with. I told you once I'm not a hearts and flowers kind of guy. I'm the idiot who takes a beautiful woman on an assault course or gets a kid stuck on top of a roller coaster but I promise, if you take a chance on me, I'll always put you first. I'll always try.'

Clara took a step closer to him, finally allowing herself to lean in against that tall, broad body, to lace her fingers around his neck, to reach up and press a kiss on that firm mouth. 'I know you will,' she whispered. 'You always put everyone else first. And I don't need hearts or flowers or clean and tidy adventure-free dates. I just need you, Raff Rafferty.'

* * * * *

Mills & Boon® Hardback

October 2014

ROMANCE

An Heiress for His Empire	Lucy Monroe
His for a Price	Caitlin Crews
Commanded by the Sheikh	Kate Hewitt
The Valquez Bride	Melanie Milburne
The Uncompromising Italian	Cathy Williams
Prince Hafiz's Only Vice	Susanna Carr
A Deal Before the Altar	Rachael Thomas
Rival's Challenge	Abby Green
The Party Starts at Midnight	Lucy King
Your Bed or Mine?	Joss Wood
Turning the Good Girl Bad	Avril Tremayne
Breaking the Bro Code	Stefanie London
The Billionaire in Disguise	Soraya Lane
The Unexpected Honeymoon	Barbara Wallace
A Princess by Christmas	Jennifer Faye
His Reluctant Cinderella	Jessica Gilmore
One More Night with Her Desert Prince...	Jennifer Taylor
From Fling to Forever	Avril Tremayne

MEDICAL

It Started with No Strings...	Kate Hardy
Flirting with Dr Off-Limits	Robin Gianna
Dare She Date Again?	Amy Ruttan
The Surgeon's Christmas Wish	Annie O'Neil

Mills & Boon® Large Print
October 2014

ROMANCE

Ravelli's Defiant Bride	Lynne Graham
When Da Silva Breaks the Rules	Abby Green
The Heartbreaker Prince	Kim Lawrence
The Man She Can't Forget	Maggie Cox
A Question of Honour	Kate Walker
What the Greek Can't Resist	Maya Blake
An Heir to Bind Them	Dani Collins
Becoming the Prince's Wife	Rebecca Winters
Nine Months to Change His Life	Marion Lennox
Taming Her Italian Boss	Fiona Harper
Summer with the Millionaire	Jessica Gilmore

HISTORICAL

Scars of Betrayal	Sophia James
Scandal's Virgin	Louise Allen
An Ideal Companion	Anne Ashley
Surrender to the Viking	Joanna Fulford
No Place for an Angel	Gail Whitiker

MEDICAL

200 Harley Street: Surgeon in a Tux	Carol Marinelli
200 Harley Street: Girl from the Red Carpet	Scarlet Wilson
Flirting with the Socialite Doc	Melanie Milburne
His Diamond Like No Other	Lucy Clark
The Last Temptation of Dr Dalton	Robin Gianna
Resisting Her Rebel Hero	Lucy Ryder

Mills & Boon® Hardback

November 2014

ROMANCE

A Virgin for His Prize	Lucy Monroe
The Valquez Seduction	Melanie Milburne
Protecting the Desert Princess	Carol Marinelli
One Night with Morelli	Kim Lawrence
To Defy a Sheikh	Maisey Yates
The Russian's Acquisition	Dani Collins
The True King of Dahaar	Tara Pammi
Rebel's Bargain	Annie West
The Million-Dollar Question	Kimberly Lang
Enemies with Benefits	Louisa George
Man vs. Socialite	Charlotte Phillips
Fired by Her Fling	Christy McKellen
The Twelve Dates of Christmas	Susan Meier
At the Chateau for Christmas	Rebecca Winters
A Very Special Holiday Gift	Barbara Hannay
A New Year Marriage Proposal	Kate Hardy
A Little Christmas Magic	Alison Roberts
Christmas with the Maverick Millionaire	Scarlet Wilson

MEDICAL

Playing the Playboy's Sweetheart	Carol Marinelli
Unwrapping Her Italian Doc	Carol Marinelli
A Doctor by Day...	Emily Forbes
Tamed by the Renegade	Emily Forbes

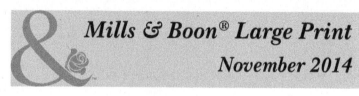

Mills & Boon® Large Print

November 2014

ROMANCE

Christakis's Rebellious Wife	Lynne Graham
At No Man's Command	Melanie Milburne
Carrying the Sheikh's Heir	Lynn Raye Harris
Bound by the Italian's Contract	Janette Kenny
Dante's Unexpected Legacy	Catherine George
A Deal with Demakis	Tara Pammi
The Ultimate Playboy	Maya Blake
Her Irresistible Protector	Michelle Douglas
The Maverick Millionaire	Alison Roberts
The Return of the Rebel	Jennifer Faye
The Tycoon and the Wedding Planner	Kandy Shepherd

HISTORICAL

A Lady of Notoriety	Diane Gaston
The Scarlet Gown	Sarah Mallory
Safe in the Earl's Arms	Liz Tyner
Betrayed, Betrothed and Bedded	Juliet Landon
Castle of the Wolf	Margaret Moore

MEDICAL

200 Harley Street: The Proud Italian	Alison Roberts
200 Harley Street: American Surgeon in London	Lynne Marshall
A Mother's Secret	Scarlet Wilson
Return of Dr Maguire	Judy Campbell
Saving His Little Miracle	Jennifer Taylor
Heatherdale's Shy Nurse	Abigail Gordon

MILLS & BOON®

Why shop at millsandboon.co.uk?

Each year, thousands of romance readers find their perfect read at millsandboon.co.uk. That's because we're passionate about bringing you the very best romantic fiction. Here are some of the advantages of shopping at www.millsandboon.co.uk:

* **Get new books first**—you'll be able to buy your favourite books one month before they hit the shops

* **Get exclusive discounts**—you'll also be able to buy our specially created monthly collections, with up to 50% off the RRP

* **Find your favourite authors**—latest news, interviews and new releases for all your favourite authors and series on our website, plus ideas for what to try next

* **Join in**—once you've bought your favourite books, don't forget to register with us to rate, review and join in the discussions

Visit **www.millsandboon.co.uk**
for all this and more today!